NORM AND LIG'S
EPIC ADVENTURE

A novel by John Goodwin
Illustrated by Adrian Waygood

Norm & Dig's Epic Adventure

Written by
John Goodwin.
Illustrated by
Adrian Waygood.

Paperback Edition
Published November 2018
ISBN 978-1-9997204-7-6

Acknowledgements

John and Adrian would like to thank their wives, Jean and Anita,

for their patience and support throughout this project.

A special thanks to Teresa Elliot as ever for help in the final edit.

Contents

Urland.

It is a well-known fact that there are two continents; Urland and Uverland. Urland, being the cradle of civilisation, is where our story starts. This it does in the hope that it will not end in Uverland as this, as everyone knows, is a place of dark foreboding.

 "The world is flat. Everyone knows that.' Norman Knocker was arguing with his lifelong friend Digby Dingle.

 'But I read it in Private Eye, which is a well-respected magazine for spies and opticians.' Digby's handsome but wart endowed face glowed with enthusiasm. 'If you cross the land in any direction you must reach the sea, right?' Norman replied, his sincere expression accentuated his bulging eyeballs. 'And when you cross the sea you eventually go over a waterfall, right?' he paused for effect. 'That, my friend, is the edge of the world.' His heavy ginger eyebrows rose to divide his forehead halfway between the top of his flat nose and his receding hairline.

'But this bloke *Arden Anonymous* said he went all the way around the world and came back on the other side of the land.'

'You are so gullible sometimes, Dig. How can you trust what a spy says, they are notorious liars?'

'How do you know he's a spy?'

'Hello?' Norman tapped his friends head with a spoon, 'with a name like that?'

'I suppose *Arden* is a bit spy-ish. Anyway, the crew of his ship bore him out.'

'Were they interviewed as well then?'

'Don't be daft; everyone knows that Sailors can't talk.'

'What about the Captain?'

'He refuses to say anything until he gets paid; it's all there in the article.'

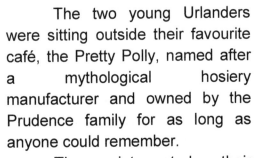

The two young Urlanders were sitting outside their favourite café, the Pretty Polly, named after a mythological hosiery manufacturer and owned by the Prudence family for as long as anyone could remember.

They interrupted their conversation with frequent sips of their preferred drink, an infusion of iron filings in hot water known as Rust Tea, which they slurped up through bendy straws. The refreshments were brought to their table by the proprietor's daughter, Prudence Prudence, a name to inspire rebellion in any girl, but most attractive for all that. The same age as the two boys, she had spent her summer holidays working in the teashop ever since she was twelve. This year, her best friend Sally Swift, a girl who always managed to live up to her name, assisted her. The two girls vied with each other for the opportunity to attend the boys' table. This did not go unnoticed and made for excellent service.

Norman and Digby had graduated from Six O'clock High and were idling away the summer before starting Uni in the autumn. It was early in the day and the summer sun cast the shadow of the town hall spire towards the nine o'clock district.

All towns in Urland had a town hall in the exact centre with a spire which had to be tall enough to cast a shadow to the farthest suburb. Each district was named after the hour in which the shadow fell on it. Therefore, if you knew what time it was, you could tell where you were. Furthermore, if you knew where you were, you could tell what time it was.

'Oh look, there's Professor Ramekin.' Digby pointed at a stooped and rustic gentleman across the road.

'Don't call out.' Norman grabbed his friend's arm. 'Too late, he's seen us. Now we're in for a half hour lecture on astronomy.'

'Don't you like astronomy?'

'Not in the holidays. I had enough at school.'

'He's coming across.'

Most Urlanders walked leaning backwards a little; this posture had evolved due to their constant quest to know what time it was, where they were, or both. However, the professor, in common with his distinguished colleagues on the faculty, was forced to lean forward due to the weight of knowledge stored in the wart on his chin. This tended to pull his face forward and make him look down on things. It had the convenient side effect of enabling him to see any obstructions on the ground, so he did not fall over as much as the less educated citizens tended to. However, it was pointless to ask him for directions, or what time it was.

'Hello boys, enjoying the holidays?' The professor peered at them over his enormous wart that gave the impression that he had a spare head tucked under his chin. All Urlanders stored their academic knowledge in a wart on their face so the extent of their education was quite apparent; most convenient for job interviews.

Norman was, at this time of his life, endowed with a wart the size of a small grape, while Digby had two smaller ones. Sometimes he thought this tended to make him a little schizophrenic, at other times he was in two minds about it.

'Hi Professor, we were just discussing the rumour that the world is round.'

'In astronomical terms, given the fact that Urland is located at the rotational pole, it is theoretically possible . . .'

'Do you have the time for some tea, Prof?' Norman interrupted the professor before he could get into his stride.

'Er . . . what time is it?' The elderly academic struggled to raise his head above horizontal.

'Nearly ten,' Norman lied.

'Oh my, I should be at the observatory by now. I'm sorry boys, why don't you write me a paper on it.' Head down, he headed down the road. At first in the wrong direction then, at shouted directions from the boys, he turned and bustled away towards the Seven O'clock district.

'Well I bet it's not true.' Norman was still chuckling as he returned to their topic.

'Well I bet it is and I'll prove it,' said Digby.

'Well how're you going to do that?'

'Well first I am going to stop starting every sentence with well and second I'll take a ship and follow the same course.'

'That may prove it to you,' said Norman, stroking his wart for the first time that day. 'But how will it prove it to me?'

'Because you are coming with me!'

So began. Norm and Dig's epic adventure.

Floating Islands.

Having, with great difficulty, persuaded their parents to allow them to take a year out before continuing their education, Norm and Dig leased a modest vessel, The Lexi. It came complete with a Captain who claimed to be conversant with wind, waves and watery matters, a Mate who also acted as head cook and assistant back scratcher and a crew of sixteen green furred Sailors who operated the oars.

'I hope this trip works out. We've spent half our tuition fund on hiring this floating coffin.' Norman leaned his tall, slim frame against the rail at the stern of the little craft watching the land they knew disappear into the distance. Above them, a family of blue crows circled their little house at the top of the mast and called raucous goodbyes to their land locked cousins.

'Of course it will.' Digby stroked the warty nodule on his right cheek. 'If we prove it is possible to circumnavigate the globe we'll be almost as famous as Mr Anonymous and if we prove it's not we'll be more famous.' Digby was several centimetres shorter than his friend but heavier built.

'What if we prove nothing?'

'Then,' said Digby, fingering the lump on his left cheek, 'we'll just be anonymous and broke.'

'If we write a paper for the professor we will be in the top of the class when we get back,' said Norm.

'If we get back.' his friend replied, still stroking his left side and then, switching to the right, he said, 'I have started a journal; I am calling it *There and Back Again.*'

'I think that's been done,' said Norm, 'but it will do for now I suppose.'

Digby pulled from his pocket an already dog-eared school exercise book and the stub of a pencil.

'Just for the record, what do you think of the ship?' he asked, licking the lead point.

'It's a bit small for my liking but it seems to have all the necessary bits.'

'And how about the Captain?'

'I'm not too sure about him. He is a Righty of course and they tend to be a bit rash.'

'I think you have to be a bit rash to undertake any sea journey, let alone a trip to the edge of the world.' Digby was favouring his left side again.

There are two kinds of Urlanders; those with their wart on the left side of their face, who tended to be rather conservative and those with it on the right side, who were more outgoing.' Norman was a Lefty, as was Knobby the Mate. Digby was a rare exception.

'Yo ho ho,' said the Captain, interrupting them. 'What's all this then?'

'Nothing,' said Digby, snapping the exercise book shut. 'Just making some notes on the journey . . . er, what's our heading?'

'What's our heading . . . what?'

'Er . . . what's our heading please, Captain Sir?' Digby had been put in his place before with regard to the correct way to address the skipper.

'That is better. Must have discipline aboard ship you know.'

'Yes, right... well what is it Captain Sir?' Norman put in.

'We follow our shadow just like the Anonymous party, but first we have to negotiate the channel between those two Islands and they are closing together fast.'

The coast of Urland is dotted with floating Islands consisting of great thicknesses of floating vegetation, which detach themselves from the land and drift out to the edge of the planet, eventually to fall over the great waterfall to oblivion.

Sometime in the distant past a troupe of great green apes became trapped on one of these organic bergs and, in fear of being swept away with it, developed the ability to row and thus resist the drift. Over generations of evolutionary development these one-hundred and fifty kilo green furred creatures populated many emerging islands and created an ever-changing seascape with their random paddling. It is from the ranks of these gentle creatures that Urlanders recruited the Sailors for their ships.

When chance brought two of the floating communities within sight of one another, each rowed as fast as they could to bring the two Islands together. When this happened, the resident apes held a big party, weddings were conducted, distant relatives were reunited and a joyous time was had by all. The festivities could go on for days.

'I think the crew have got a sniff of the others and are slowing down so that we have to join the party.' Captain Ali frowned.

'What can we do, Captain?' Digby asked.

'I've sent the mate to jolly them up with a good scratching but he could do with a hand,'

'How do we do that?'

'Just take a couple of back scratchers and give them a scratch between the shoulder blades; that should do the trick.'

Norm and Dig took up the rough wooden implements, clambered down to the oar deck and set to work. Each ape wriggled and writhed in delight as their turn came but they kept on rowing. When the boys came up the Captain was at the wheel and the floating Islands were close on each side.

'I think we will just make it, me hearties,' the Captain called.

He was wrong. Just as the channel began to open up in front of them, the oars caught on a section of weed below the water and they shuddered to a halt. Their craft was soon swallowed up by the surrounding vegetation.

Grounded.

As luck would have it, the two converging masses slid under the curved hull and lifted it without crushing its sides. It now sat high and dry  about a hundred metres from the water's edge. In no time at all it was surrounded by the excited whooping residents of the two Islands.

They, however, were not the slightest bit interested in the ship or its passengers. They rushed to greet their contemporaries from the other group. Many had prepared in advance by weaving large and gaudy blossoms in their fur. All but one of the Sailors from the ship had swarmed over the side as soon as it stopped and disappeared into the throng. The final one now followed at a more leisurely pace, a bright red blossom behind its ear.

Norm and Dig stood with the Captain and Mate at the ships rail. They watched as the excitement among the natives reached fever pitch. The wild and random whooping and hollering coalesced into a regular rhythm. Some of the members started stamping their feet and, as others joined the dance, the ground began to undulate in time. Hundreds of heavy green creatures, all bouncing up and down together, caused the vegetable matting to rise and fall as if it was the very ocean itself.

The ship rocked from side to side and, for the first time since leaving port, Norman declared he felt seasick.

'Knobby,' the Captain addressed the Mate. 'Go and fetch my bottle from the cabin, will you?'

'Ay ay Sir,' the Mate who happened to be called Knobby Knocker was no relation to Norman. It was the fashion to name your children with the same initials to the first name as the surname; Knobby's family had a more fundamentalist view of the use of the silent "K" than Norman's.

'A swig of this will fix you up,' the Captain said when the Mate returned. He took a swig himself before handing the large yellow bottle to the youngster whose colour was beginning to resemble that of the apes.

'Er . . . what is it?' Norm sniffed at its neck. 'Smell's fishy.'

'Aha, get it down yer me hearty; it'll do ye good.' The Captain was not in the habit of talking like that but he felt that a few 'yo ho hos' and the occasional 'Avast there me hearty' made him sound more seaman like. In fact, he was an accountant by profession. He became fed up with always being the bearer of bad news. (Accountant's reports are always bad news). So one day he gave it all up and went to sea on a whim. After a while he graduated to a Wherry, until he bought the Lexi and declared himself Captain.

Norm took a swig, and his complexion began to take on the colour of the bottle.

'Cod Liver Oil,' he exclaimed. 'Good stuff too.' He took another draught. 'Boy that's got a kick.'

'Here, give us swig.' Digby reached for the bottle.

'Medicinal purposes only!' the Captain intercepted the pass, took a swallow, then wiped the neck with his thumb and rubbed the residue onto his wart. Pounding the stopper back into place in a manner that left no doubts as to its finality, he slipped the bottle into the pocket of his jacket.

'I'm afraid there is nothing we can do for now lads. I suggest we get slicked up and join the party.'

'Yeah, party on.' Norman was a somewhat intoxicated already. The little group dispersed to their individual cabins to prepare for the festivities.

The Lexi was once an Urland Postal Service ship called, as they all were, Lexicon. They were all built to a very high standard using the finest hardwood planking and replaced every five years or so. Each new craft was given the next number in turn. This particular vessel was previously known as Lexicon 2. When you consider the latest one to join the fleet was Lexicon 35 it will give you some idea of its age. All were blessed with the same design having the Post Master and Captain's quarters at the stern with the galley and mess. There was space for four postmen in the bow with the rowing deck in between. Below the rowing deck was the hold. This was divided into three rows of bins marked alphabetically. For the purposes of the circumnavigation expedition, these compartments had been stuffed full of provisions.

Unknown to the adventurers a strange thing was starting to happen in compartment 'S'. Listed on the manifest as twenty sacks of brussels sprouts, one of the hessian bags had started to show movement from within. This was unlikely to be discovered because, although Urlanders would eat or drink almost anything, most drew the line at sprouts, so the bin would be expected to remain undisturbed until they were starving to death.

Shore Party

The initial exuberance of the joining celebrations had died down by the time the adventurers reassembled on deck. Captain Ali Anxious, a good name for an accountant, looked very dashing in his dress uniform; a dark blue tail coat over white, naval pattern bell bottom trouser above which could clearly be seen his hairy belly button. Gold epaulettes shone on his shoulders and his left cuff was strewn with scrambled egg, a remnant of his breakfast no doubt. He wore a feathered three-cornered hat which he doffed in greeting, revealing that his normally wild flowing hair had been slicked down and parted in the middle, not only front to back but also side to side. The four corners tidied into plaits tied with white cord at the ends. He smelt strongly of cod liver oil and mothballs.

Knobby had put on a clean blue and white striped crop-top and white shorts similar to the ones he always wore. His red hair, normally tied in a ponytail at the back, now hung fetchingly in a bunch to the side of his face partially obscuring one eye. It clearly annoyed him as he kept blowing it back out of the way from the corner of his mouth but as he said when asked, 'That's the price of beauty.'

Norman had put on his best grey suit, complete with silk brocade waistcoat and a white silk scarf flowing from his neck.

It was Digby, however, that stole the show. Last to arrive, he strode onto the deck resplendent in a bright yellow tropical suit complete with shoes and socks to match. The outfit was topped off with an oversized pith helmet' resplendent with a trail of exotic multicoloured feathers which made even the Captain's ostrich plumes seem limp and drab.

'Ready to go?' he said casually as he leaned over the rail for better view of the party. 'Er . . . how'd we get down?' They were a good six metres from the ground.

'Fetch the ladder Mr Mate,' the Captain roared. 'We're a going ashore! Oh, and batten down the hatches on the way out'.

After the initial knees up the inhabitants had settled down to what, for them, would be considered a genteel cocktail party. Food and drink had been brought and laid out on mats of palm leaves and, using half coconut shells as cups, they mingled, looked for long-lost friends or relatives and made new acquaintances. The younger ones started looking for mates.

Digby was immediately adopted by a large female who had taken a fancy to his headgear. She scooped him up

 and, despite his cries for help, carried him away to the nearest palm tree which she nimbly climbed. Settled in its branches she sat the young Urlander on her knee like some erstwhile ventriloquist's dummy and fed him bananas.

Norm, Knobby and Captain Anxious, when they stopped laughing, helped themselves to the buffet. Norm was particularly taken with the salad, which was dressed with an oily substance that he had not tasted before. It gave the leaves an added piquancy that he found quite delicious.

'Hey Dig,' he called to his friend, 'you should try this, it's great.'

'I'll be right down.' Digby squirmed in the gentle but unyielding grip of the ape. 'Or maybe not.' He was really full of banana now and she was already peeling another one with her feet.

'Ahoy up there,' the Captain laughed, 'If you give her your hat she might let you go.'

'My beautiful hat? Never!' Digby managed to say before another fifteen centimetres of fruit was stuffed into his mouth.

'It's up to you.' The Captain shrugged and pointedly peeled a banana of his own. Digby looked down at his hostess's feet; they were already at work on the next one. He took off his treasured headgear, gave it one last look and offered it to her.

Delighted, the creature took the gift with both hands, completely forgetting about her young charge. Without warning, Digby plummeted to the ground, landing with a thump on the soft earth. For several moments he lay like a smashed egg on the ferny floor. When he got his breath back he clambered to his feet. His friends had gathered around, their initial concern turned to side-splitting laughter when they realised he was all right.

'Why me?' Digby moaned as he brushed himself off.

'I could tell you but it might be better if I show you,' said the Captain. 'Come with me.'

'Would you like a banana to eat on the way?' Norman laughed as they followed Anxious into the undergrowth. After a few minutes trek in the thickening vegetation the Captain stopped and signalled them to be quiet. They went forward on all fours until quite suddenly the jungle stopped and they found themselves looking down into a wide bowl of flattened leaves.

'You might have warned me.' Digby exclaimed.

'Ssh,' the Captain hissed and pointed across the clearing. A huge female gorilla stood up and sniffed the air suspiciously. The men quickly withdrew but she saw the movement and charged, stepping across the nest with speed and care that belied her bulk. Her young charges, yellow furred young apes, shrieked in alarm and huddled behind her. The Urlanders fled, fleet footed Knobby in the lead and Captain Anxious breathlessly bringing up the rear. They made it to the party site and, in the absence of any sound of pursuit, fell to the ground alongside the picnic spread. They all took a drink of water from the Pitcher-plants that had been laid out on a wicker tray. The liquid was spiced with insects that the plant had captured, each one having a distinct flavour. They swapped cups so that each could savour the others. All agreed that they were very refreshing and,

suitably rejuvenated, they re-joined the party. Dancing had begun again and they were soon caught up in the rhythm, whirling and stomping with the best of them. As a precaution, Digby shed his jacket revealing his white silk  under shirt. Occasionally, across the crowded space he caught a glimpse of his feathered bonnet bobbing about in the ocean of green fur that surrounded him.

Head Banging

Norm was the first to wake. He found himself sitting with his back against the rudder of the stranded ship. Alongside him were his fellow travellers in various positions of repose. Digby, spread eagled and doing his best impression of a fried egg, lay next to Knobby who was face down, his tee shirt pulled over his head. The Captain lay on his side curled into a ball with his thumb wedged firmly in his mouth.

Norm stood up and stretched, thrusting out his arms and, twisting his head from side to side, his neck clicked loudly in protest. They had kept up with the frenzied dancing until they dropped. Too exhausted to climb the ladder back to their cabins, they spent the night on the soft, warm, slightly undulating ground. Like a giant waterbed, it had lulled them to sleep.

Norm, accidently on purpose, kicked Dig's outstretched leg.

'Wha...' Digby began his struggle for consciousness. 'Where?' He was so articulate first thing in the day.

'Oh, you are awake then,' Norm observed casually as if he had been up for hours.

'Oh, you are awake then,' Norm observed casually, as if he had been up for hours.

'No.' his friend replied sullenly. 'What time is it?'

'I can't tell, we will have to climb up and check the compass.'

Urlander ships were like giant sundials with a mast at the centre acting like the town hall spire on land. They had been equipped with canvas sails at one time so that they could cast a more distinct shadow, but this was found to resist the efforts of the rowers if the wind was in the wrong direction so the idea was dropped. Because the ship could be pointed in any direction, time keeping was somewhat a hit and miss affair until the compass was invented.

The others were beginning to stir now and Digby, wandering around to loosen his limbs, made a discovery that delighted him no end. There, balanced on a stalk of fresh green bananas, was his beloved hat.

'Just look at this,' he exclaimed.

'Say that again, I didn't see your lips move,' Norman addressed the bananas, which were also wearing Digby's jacket.

'Don't make me, laugh my head is pounding,' Dig retrieved his apparel.

'We really should avoid insect water in future. It is more intoxicating than cod liver oil,' the Captain said, sitting up and rubbing his brow. 'Let's get back on board, I need a drink. Mr Mate, avast there!'

Knobby moaned but did not move. The Captain bent over the recumbent figure and yelled in his ear,

'All hands on deck!' He then reeled backwards clutching his head, muttering, 'Never again.'

Knobby leapt to his feet and looked all around blinking like a startled rabbit.

'What is it, pirates?' he stumbled about still unaware of his surroundings.

'Just get yourself on deck Mr Mate, and bring those bananas with you.'

Digby groaned at the thought of more bananas on board, he had definitely overdosed on them the night before.

The sorry group clambered up the ladder and sat around the table in the aft cabin which acted as a mess. Knobby was detailed to make breakfast and over a light meal of banana omelettes, they discussed their situation.

'Of course the Islands might split right here and we will be deposited back in the sea again, it does happen sometimes.' He generously passed one of his precious bottles of cod liver oil around for a livener and they started to feel better.

'But our Sailors have gone AWOL.' Norman pointed out, stroking his wart.

'Perhaps we could talk them into coming back,' said Digby, fiddling with his right cheek. 'Although I doubt that we could make ourselves understood' he stroked his left.

The oceanic apes only had two basic sounds in their vocabulary, Hoo and Eee, although apparently there were thousands of nuances of inflection that no Urlander had ever fathomed. Their concept of language was therefore somewhat limited. For instance, like their landlocked cousins, the Roadies, they could only count to two. Hoo, equalled one, but also meant yes, good, in, and hello, whereas eee, meant, two, no, bad, out, and goodbye.

'The other problem is finding them. There was not a single ape in sight when we came on board,' the Captain pointed out.

Digby slumped, resting his head on the table resignedly; the others sat in glum silence.

'You know,' Digby said at length, 'I thought the pounding in my head had gone away but I feel it coming back now.'

'Impossible, said the Captain examining the contents of the bottle through the glass. 'That cod liver oil you just swigged half a bottle of is guaranteed to cure all known ills, up to and including a broken leg.'

'But there is a distinct thumping.' He raised his head to look at them. 'It's stopped, hang on.' He put his head down on the table again. 'It's coming from here.'

They all put their heads down. Once the echoes of cranium on timber died away, they all detected a distinct thumping sound.

Knobby dropped to the floor and pressed his ear to the planking.

'It's coming from the hold.' He tapped with his hairy knuckles. 'I can hear yelling; someone's in there.'

'Come on boys, open the hatch.' Knobby ran forward and started throwing the bolts. The Captain helped him lift the heavy cover while Norm and Dig peered into the void.

The assault that came from within the hold was unprecedented in maritime history.

Stowaways

Norman was pinned to the mast by the force of Sally's rush as she lived up to her name and sallied forth.

'How dare you go to a party and leave us locked in that smelly hold all night,' she screeched.

'But I . . .'

'Don't you but me Norman Knocker,' she yelled into his face.

'But we . . .'

'Don't blame them; it's you I'm talking to.' She was not in the mood for logic.

'Where did you come from?' Digby tried to intervene.

'You keep out of this Digby Dingle. I'll deal with you later. Well Norman, what have you got to say for yourself?' The tirade went on.

Relieved not to be the focus of Sally Swift's attention, Digby turned to Prudence who was standing in the hatchway, tears rolling down her cheek.

'What's going on?' he asked

'You went to a party without us,' she explained through her sobs. 'We went to all the trouble of stowing away and the first party you go to you lock us in.' Her makeup was running in green rivulets down her cheeks. 'We spent the night all gussied up with nowhere to go and it's all your fault.'

'But we didn't know you were there,' Digby protested.

'Well you should have done.' Prudence collapsed into Digby's arms as if that was the end of the matter.

Sally and Norman's conversation had degenerated into a snogging session that was also without precedent in maritime history. The Captain and Mate busied themselves with the hatch and politely pretended not to notice.

When the two couples eventually untangled their limbs, they joined the crew in the mess for a conference.

'Do your parents know where you are?,' was the Captain's first question.

'Do you know where we are?' was Sally's stinging repost.

'Well . . . no, but that is not the issue,' the Captain replied.

'I left a note,' said Prudence in an effort to diffuse the tension.

'And if you can tell me exactly where I am I'll send an email.' Sally could not resist pressing the point.

'In my note I said you were coming with me,' said Prudence. 'Can we do email from here?'

'Nope,' said Knobby. 'We have to use ship to shore.'

'How does that work?' said Sally

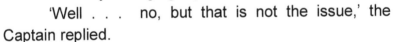

'We just take the ship to the shore and send a note,' laughed the mate.

On land, the email system involved a team of trained eagles which were used to transfer messages from one area to another. To send an E message, it was necessary to write it down and place it in a string bag known as the inter-net, which was then taken to the nearest eagle's eyrie. This was a dangerous job for little reward so those who carried it out were known as Idiot Service Providers (ISPs). The Eagle was given the scent of the nearest nest to the destination. It would then fly there and drop off the net. This would then be recovered by another ISP and delivered to the recipient's door. The whole process could take a day or two and those who used the service were always complaining about the internet speed. In general it was easier to telephone.

'Well that is out of the question,' said the Digby. 'At the moment we are high and dry with no Sailors to row us.'

'What I want to know is, how did you get on board?' the Captain demanded.

'We hid in a couple of crates,' said Prudence 'and waited until the dockers loaded us into the hold.'

'Was there anything in the crates?' Captain Anxious asked anxiously.

'Just some bottles, but we took them out first of course.'

'Double entry double dealings!' the Captain exclaimed, 'My cod-liver oil!'

'What?' said Digby.

'Er... I mean... shiver me timbers, what a disaster. We can't get another supply out here. We're marooned without a drink! Marooned I tell ye Jim lad.' He'd heard that last bit in a play.

'Who?' said Digby.

'Hoo, hoo, hoo, hoo, hoo.' The sound was coming from the rowing deck.

'It's the Sailors,' called Knobby from the cabin door, 'they're back. Quick, get your back scratchers and follow me.'

They all set to, even the Captain, and they soon had a satisfied complement of rowers. All the positions were filled except for one. They were just finishing the last back when they heard a cry from the shore.

'Ahoy there, permission to come aboard!'

They ran to the rail to be met by an amazing sight; there below was a scrawny looking Urlander. He was dressed faded and frayed seaman's garb and was dragging a small crate behind him.

'Who be you, you lubber?' the Captain called in his most seaman-like manner.

'If you please Captain, Sir, I be called Ben Bun. I bin stranded 'ere these last ten years. Ye wouldn't have a bit o' cheese would ye.'

'I might,' the Captain replied. 'But why should I give any to you?'

'Have a little charity, Captain Sir. I only wish for a little cheese, some civilised conversation and maybe join your crew to sail away from this primitive place.'

'I have all the crew I need and we are embarked on a long voyage. We need all the provisions we have including the cheese.' was the Captain's terse reply.

'Ye won't be a goin' far from this position will ye,' Ben Bun said a sly look on his face.

'I admit we are a little stuck at the moment,' said the Captain.

'I can help ye there . . . In exchange for maybe a little cheese.'

Suddenly Prudence appeared in the Captain's line of sight. She was carrying a plate of bread and cheese.

'Prudence, stay back,' the Captain called in alarm.

'There you are my dear fellow,' she said, handing the scrawny wretch the food. He snatched it from her and ate greedily. Through teeth sticking together with bread and cheese he said,

'Thank ye kindly ma'am.' He continued to munch his way through half a kilo of cheese and three crusty rolls. When he was finished, he looked back up at the Captain.

'If ye want my help I'll give it to you Cap'n.'

'What can you do?' the Captain asked.

'Let me aboard and I'll tell you,' Ben replied.

'Go on Captain. What harm can it do??,' Prudence called up as she retrieved the empty plate.

'Er... what is in the crate?' the Captain asked suspiciously.

'All me worldly goods, a few scraps of clothes, a couple of charts and half a case of cod-liver-oil.

'Well in that case, come aboard,' said the Captain.

Ben's Tale

Once Ben was seated at the mess table with another plate of bread and cheese, Captain Anxious pressed the newcomer for an explanation as to how he came to be on the floating Island.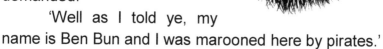

'Who are you and what are you doing here?' he demanded.

'Well as I told ye, my name is Ben Bun and I was marooned here by pirates.'

'Pirates, w.... what pirates?' Norman asked nervously stroking his wart.

'So ye were a pirate were ye, aye, ahaar, ye swab,' the Captain was triggered into going over the top in his use of pseudo-seaman language at the mention of the scourge of the sea-lanes.

'Aye, well, no well...' Ben reddened. 'Perhaps I should start at the beginning.' He took a mouthful of cheese and reached for the bottle of cod liver oil, which the Captain moved out of range. Then, through lips sticky with part-chomped comestibles, the castaway went on.

'I first went to sea in a post vessel somewhat like this,' he said, spraying the table and surrounding company with damp crumbs.

'Here, drink this.' Prudence handed him a cup of water and proceeded to wipe the table with a cloth, unable to deny her waitressing instincts.

'Ok,' she said at last, 'do go on.'

'I was only a nipper, quite a bit younger than you fine gentlemen at the time. I ran away to sea even though I was from a good family of bakers.'

'Hence the name Ben Bun,' Digby interjected.

'Not quite young Sir,' Ben replied, 'my real name is Kieran Kipling.'

'Wow, not the long-lost heir to the famous Kipling family fortune,' said Sally. 'They make exceedingly good cakes you know.'

'Unfortunately not. I am from the other side of the family; we made ruddy-hard cakes.'

'Ahaar,' said the Captain. 'I've heard of them, the Rudyard Kipling's, the bane of the catering trade and delight of the dentist profession. But get on with it man. How came ye here.'

'I was coming to that,' Ben went on, the remains of his sandwich clutched unbitten in his hand.

'I changed my name to escape the scandal and signed on as a cabin boy in the long distance postal service. The ship was called the Lexicon 26, ahaar, she was the newest ship in the fleet, aye, and a very fine craft she were too. I learned the ropes from an old sea dog called Argent; he was, at the time, the ship's cook. He had a squinty eye and only one leg, the other one was replaced with the leg of a table and he had to keep his balance with a crutch made from whalebones.

'We sailed together for several years then, just before one Wintermas when the ship was laden with expensive gifts, Argent led a mutiny and took over the ship. He put the officers and postal workers in a long boat and cast them adrift. I wanted to go with them but Captain Argent, as he dubbed himself, insisted I stay. He said that, as it was the rock cakes I had made that were used to lay the captain low, I would be strung up as a mutineer when they reached land so I was forced into the life of a pirate. Aye, he still uses my recipe for making ammunition for his cannon. Shiver me timbers matey, ye don't want to be on the receiving end of one of my rock cakes, they'll take your head right off I can tell ye, ahaar.' He took a bite of his sandwich, holding the curly corners together with his spare hand.

'So how come ye ended up here?' the Captain pressed him. Ben crammed the remains of the bread into his mouth and looked longingly at the oil bottle at the far side of the table.

'If I could just oil me clack...' Ben sprayed more crumbs around as he spoke. Prudence swiftly wiped them up.

'Ok, just a sip,' said the Captain, 'Then get to the point, ye swab. You said you could help us off this floating cabbage patch, didn't ye?'

'Oh I can and I will,' said Ben. 'But ye need to understand that I am but a victim of misfortune. Ye see that was all many years ago and Captain Argent led us on many a pirate adventure. Aye, but he didn't kill his victims outright. He always cast them adrift in a long boat equipped with a portable toilet. That is how he got his nickname, Long John Argent. Personally, I think he was a little potty himself ahaar... aye and that was me downfall. He overheard me joking about it and dumped me on a deserted clump of weed with a loaf of bread and no cheese. Luckily, my little clump was gathered up by this ape infested veggie-burger before I died of thirst and I fell in with its occupants.'

'So that is how ye ended up here,' said the Captain.

'Yes, well actually that was long ago and here wasn't here then. It was many leagues away.'

'Yes, yes, yes ye lubber, but how does that help us get back to sea.'

'Give me another swig of that oil and I'll show ye, Cap'n.' Ben stood and reached for the bottle. The Captain let him take a swig.

'Now get on with it,' he said.

'Ye see, I've lived with these critters for the past ten year, so I've picked up more than a smattering of their patois.' He commenced to hoot and screech, at first to the apes in the rowing deck then, cupping his hands around his mouth, he hollered over the side. In ones and twos at first, then in greater numbers the tribe of apes appeared out of the undergrowth and gathered alongside The Lexi. They listened with rapt attention as Ben, standing on the ships rail, addressed them in hoos and ees of complex patterns. Finally, he turned to the Urlanders gathered behind him and said, 'Ok, hold tight.' Almost at once the craft started to move.

Sea at Last, Sea at Last.

Shaken off their feet by the sudden righting of the vessel's deck they picked themselves up and ran to the rail. Only Ben had managed to maintain his stance, gripping firmly to the rigging with one hand. Partially hidden by the curve of the hull, hundreds of the green beasties were pushing the craft forward, while many more were busily rubbing the vegetation in front of them with what looked like large round shells.

'What are those apes doing?' Digby asked.

'They're lubricating the path to the sea using the slimy foot of giant snails. Jolly useful, the giant snail, not only as a lubricant but they also make a great salad dressing, ahaar,' Ben replied licking his lips.

Gradually the ship gained momentum and, once on the oiled area, its speed increased rapidly until the pushers were running to keep up. The oilers scattered from its path and, with a mighty splash, The Lexi slid into the sea. The crew members, once recovered from the soaking by the resultant deluge, ran to the stern to wave and call their thanks to their friends ashore. Many of the apes waved back, others danced and it looked like another party was about to start. However, the Sailors set to rowing and the floating island started to dwindle behind them. They were just starting to turn away when a large hairy hand gripped the rail alongside Sally making her shriek and jump back.

'Ho, ho, ho,' said the ape as it clambered up onto the poop deck.

'Hoo, eee,' Ben replied, 'don't panic young miss, it is just your missing crew member.' He turned to the others who had also taken a step back, 'Cap'n Sir, ladies and gentlemen all, ahaar. May I introduce Phd. She is the most travelled of all the great oceanic apes,'

'Pleased to make your acquaintance ma'am.' The Captain doffed his three-cornered hat in a mocking bow. The great green creature curtsied in a most elegant and graceful manner and proffered the back of her hand in a regal gesture that left the ship's skipper no option but to take it up and kiss it.

'Hoo, hoo, eee,' said Phd and lumbered off to take up her place among the rowing crew, the red flower still fresh behind her ear.

The other apes didn't break their rhythm as they called their greetings to the late arrival and she swiftly unshipped her sweep and seamlessly joined the enthusiastic rowers.

'How did you know that was Phd?' Norm asked Ben as they made their way with Dig, Sally and Prudence down to the aft cabin. 'They all look the same to me; I can't even tell if they are male or female.'

'Aye, well it is difficult even for them with all that green hair, you have to get pretty intimate to find out, ahaar.'

'I think I would sooner not know,' said Norm rubbing his wart. 'But you knew her straight away.'

'Aye well the flower was a clue; it is a rare bloom which outside of her keeping only grows in Uverland.'

'Uverland... The place of dark foreboding!' the young Urlanders exclaimed together.

'Have you been there?' Digby asked.

'Aye lad, that I have, and so has she, ahaar.'

'Oh do tell us about it, is it really scary?' Prudence asked as they gathered round the table. The Captain and mate were busy doing seaman-like things such as making sure that they were on the right heading and cleaning the poop off the poop deck. Ben, finding a receptive audience, embarked on one of his nautical tales.

'If ye travel far enough south,' he began, 'another sun appears in the sky. Not a nice golden warm sun like ours, oh no me hearties, but a big red orb that offers little heat. If ye keep ye heading, our sun disappears and everything is bathed in this cold red light. It takes a lot of courage to keep a-going I can tell ye, but if ye do ahaar, if ye can, ye will eventually reach land.'

'The land of dark foreboding,' Digby whispered.

'Aye lad, Uverland.'

'What's it like? Do tell,' Sally begged.

'It is always cold there, bitter cold and dim to the eye, ahaar. It is the place where the phrase 'shiver me timbers' was invented 'cos even the woodworm's teeth were chattering, ahaar.

I'm not sure I like the sound of that,' said Prudence, wrapping a shawl around her shoulders despite the warmth of the cabin.

'Aye, but there's worse things than the cold, ahaar,'

'All hands on deck!' the Captain's voice bellowed from above. 'Stand by to repel boarders.'

Ben leapt to his feet and grabbed a cutlass from the rack on the wall. Digby and Norman followed suit.

'You girls better stay here,' Digby called as he headed for the door.

'Not likely,' shouted Sally. She grabbed the last remaining cutlass in one hand and with a kitchen knife in the other she charged past the boys onto the deck. The sight that met them was almost beyond description.

Denizens.

The sea around the ship was boiling with large dark blue and white shapes circling them, each one breaking the surface from time to time in a flurry of foam. The Sailors in the rowing deck could not operate their sweeps and were quickly stowing them inboard.

'Stand by to repel boarders!' the Captain repeated. 'They'll be on us in a minute.'

'What will?' yelled Norman above the din of splashing water and clattering oars.

'Flying fish,' Knobby replied. 'Try to keep them from eating the rigging.' He leapt to the rail armed with a large iron chamber pot. Ben nimbly jumped up onto  the rail on the other side just as the first of the two metre long winged sharks thrust itself high out of the water alongside the slowing vessel. Ben swept his cutlass at the creature putting a slash in its tail before it crashed back into the sea. Another leapt at them, this time clearing the deck and landing in the water on the other side. Its jaws snapped repeatedly as it went revealing rows of viciously curved teeth. Then they came on thick and fast. Knobby struck one squarely on the nose with his potty sending it back the way it came. Sally charged up onto the foredeck just in time to skewer one of the fish that had landed there and was attacking one of the stays. She barely had time to kick the stricken monster through the railings when another flew at her, jaws wide enough to swallow her head. Norman was there in the nick of time and, with a mighty blow, severed the fish in two at the shoulder. The separate halves splattered to the deck still flapping and snapping accordingly. They stood back to back to face the onslaught. Digby joined the captain on the Poop and together they despatched several of the denizens over the side. Knobby and Ben batted and battered any that came within reach of their swinging weapons but could not keep many of the fierce creatures from landing among the Sailors in the open rowing deck below them. Any that arrived there were given short shrift, in a pacifistic way, by the apes. Most times, they deftly caught them by the snout, holding the jaw shut before flipping them neatly back over the side. Some they just grabbed by the tail and swung clear away. Others they gripped by their wing-like fins and tossed over the side. Never did they hurt or damage the viciously snapping adversary even in self-defence.

The onslaught went on for what seemed like hours, but gradually the airborne attacks became less frequent although the sea still boiled around them as the creatures fed on their injured comrades. The Lexi drifted slowly away leaving a red cauldron behind. Once clear, the Apes unshipped their oars and started to pull steadily, resuming their original course.

'Phew,' said the Captain. 'That was thirsty work. Ben, break out one of your bottles of oil, I think we all deserve a drink.'

'I've made a nice fresh pot of rust tea,' said Prudence appearing from the cabin, 'but you had better get cleaned up before you come in here. I have just washed the floor.' Prudence's reaction to adversity was to clean something and, in this case, the aft cabin positively gleamed.

'Fetch the oil,' Captain anxiously repeated, ignoring the girl.

'Aye aye Cap'n,' Ben replied and hurried below to cargo hold 'B' where his chest had been stored. If he had not been so tired he might have noticed that the small movements in hold 'S' had now begun in another of the sacks of sprouts. As it was, he grabbed a bottle from his locker, took a quick but deep swig, and hurried right past back on deck.

Knobby had thrown a line with a bucket on it over the side and was drawing water from the sea to wash the bloody decks. Sally was busily kicking remnants of flying shark over the side of the foredeck. Seagulls had appeared from nowhere and were circling the ship, occasionally swooping down to grab the odd piece of fish from the ocean.

'Ahoy there, young miss, don't throw it all away,' Ben shouted. 'Damn fine eating, wing of Shark. Fish and chips tonight ahaar.'

'But I've made cheese sandwiches,' said Prudence.

'Well we can have them for a snack and eat the fish later,' said Digby. 'I'm starving.' He headed for the cabin.

'Oh no you don't!' said Prudence. 'Not until you clean yourself up.'

'All hands set to,' said the Captain from the wheel. 'Clean the ship, me hearties, then the crew, then we eat.' He took a deep swig from the bottle that Ben handed him. 'Mr Mate there is a big fat fish stuck up in the rigging. Lop its wings before ye throw it over the side. There's more than enough there for a good fish supper, ahaar.'

'Aye aye Captain,' Knobby replied.

Fortified with a swig of Ben's cod liver oil all round they scrubbed the decks, then themselves and finally settled in the cabin where Prudence had laid an excellent spread of savouries with scones and tea to follow.

'Is that a common occurrence?' Digby asked as he leaned back in his chair holding his overfull stomach.

'They don't usually swim this far north,' said Ben, thoughtfully stroking his wart. 'In all my years at sea I only saw them attack a ship once.'

'What happened in that case?' said the Captain.

'Oh they ate it, crew and all.'

'Shiver me timbers!' said the Captain. 'I've heard of such a thing but I've never experienced it. I guess we were lucky aye.'

'Aye, well the trick is to get enough of them bleeding in the water, ahaar, then they turn on one another, ahaar,' Ben said sleepily. 'Now, if ye'll excuse me, I will sling me hammock and get forty winks. That was tiring work for an old seaman.'

As he came from a land that, for most of the year, was in perpetual daylight, Ben, like all Urlanders, only took occasional naps just when he felt like it, except in the three months of winter. Then everyone fell asleep when the sun went down and woke again when it rose.

'I had better set a watch for the helm,' said the Captain. 'Then we all should get some sleep.'

'Don't worry Cap'n,' said Ben. 'Phd will keep us on course and call us in an emergency.'

'All the same, we will keep a watch. Knobby you first. Call me in an hour.'

'Aye, aye, Captain, I want to go up and check up on the lookouts anyway, I haven't seen or heard from them since the attack.' Knobby gathered the few remaining scraps of food from off their plates, put them in bag and set off to climb the mast, leaving Prudence and Digby to clear the table and do the washing up. The others had quickly disappeared to bed.

Pirates.

It is a well-known fact, that blue crows use the same nest each year. As migratory birds, they go south for the winter and return to their homes in the spring to breed. Being essentially lazy creatures, it is not difficult to persuade them to nest in a place that often travels south, saving them all that flapping. Blue crows were the most vigilant of the many sub-species and would squawk and fly in circles anytime something new appeared on the horizon. This made them excellent lookouts for ships.

Knobby looked after his crows, feeding them regularly on scraps from the galley. He knew that, as they were somewhat alarmist in nature, they were inherent cowards. When he reached the top of the mast he found them huddling inside their converted barrel home. It took him most of his watch to persuade them to come out for some food. Occasionally he would stand on the roof of the crow's nest, shielding his eyes with his hand, to scan the horizon. He noticed that the sun now seemed to be sinking almost out of sight instead of running round and round like it did in Urland.

The sea was all that was visible in any direction but in the south clouds were gathering, combined with the imminent disappearance of the sun. It was as though winter was on its way early. Once the crows had returned to duty, taking it in turns for circuits and bumps, and they had settled down after discovering the ominous grey cumulus building in the distance, Knobby returned to the deck. An hour and a half had passed when he woke the Captain and gave his report.

'Well done Mr Mate,' said the Captain. 'Now call a pair of the land lubbers to take the next watch. I'm going to write this all up in my ledger.'

'You mean your Log, Sir?' Knobby corrected, taking care to remain respectful.

'Oh er...aye, that too, ahaar. Avast there now me fine bucko.' The Captain's hand swung away from the thick triple entry ledger he was reaching for and took down the slim ship's log from alongside it on the bookshelf. 'Afore ye turn in,' he said, 'get me a fix and an accurate time check will ye ahaar.'

'Aye, aye, Captain,' Knobby acknowledged as he left.

Prudence and Digby were already up when he entered the galley. Ben, supervising from his hammock slung in a corner of the room, was directing them in how to fillet the shark wings. They had managed to remove most of the meat in a dozen large cutlets and, using the soft white under-skin, were preparing to make sausages with the smaller off cuts. Being informed with much giggling that Norm and Sally were busy in their cabin, he told the other pair to come on deck as soon as they had finished with the food.

Life on board finally settled into a routine. The Captain, having written up the log, happily set about auditing the ship's accounts ready for a mid-voyage report.

The Sailors stopped rowing for an hour twice a day and disappeared over the side to forage for sea weed but otherwise rowed steadily and, it appeared, happily on their course. Each of the couples was instructed in how to tell if the crows had spotted anything. They took turns on watch during the day, with Knobby and Ben making the duty crew for the night shift, which soon extended to eight hours. Like all creatures in Urland, the crows slept through the hours of darkness so a vigilant Urlander eye was required at these times. A few oil lamps were on board but there were no navigation lights as the vessel was never intended to sail in the winter months or leave the coastal waters.

The dark clouds that had gathered to the south had gradually extended to the horizon all around them but they sailed blissfully through the gentle swell. It was against the murky background that, in the pre-dawn light, Knobby's sharp eyes spotted a tiny dark blip.

He climbed the mast to get a better view, waking the crows in passing. The crows had much better long vision than people and were soon milling around and shrieking blue murder (hence a murder of crows). Alerted by the din, the Captain strode on deck, an anxious look on his face.

'Avast there, Mr Mate' he called 'what ye see?'

'A ship, a ship with sails set!' Knobby replied.

'Where away?' Captain Anxious was pleased to have remembered the phrase from his Seaman's Manual. Digby pointed to the south.

'Sally, get my spy glass from the cabin, will ye?' The captain sprang to the foredeck for a better look. 'Ben, get the Sailors to stop rowing, take a rest and an early breakfast. We may need full speed later.'

'Aye, aye, Cap'n,' Ben peered into the gloom of the well deck and eee'd and hoo'd for a bit. Phd joined him at the rail, took one look, then hooted a quick command at her comrades. They swarmed over the side to feed then came back quickly, each clutching great bunches of kelp in both hands.

Through his spyglass the captain focused on the blip. 'I can see it, black sails but I can't make out the flag.'

'Hogwash!' said Ben.

'No really, black sails,' said the Captain. 'Take a look for ye-self ye swab.' Ben took the glass and pointed it at the distant object.

'Like I said, Hogwash,' he said taking the lens from his eye. 'Captain Horatio Hogwash. The only man more ruthless and cruel than Long John Argent.' At this Phd, who had followed him up on deck, started hooing and eeing and hopping up and down in a most excited fashion.

'Hoo hoo hoo,' she said pointing towards the rising sun.

'She wants us to go east Cap'n,' Ben interpreted.

'No, that's into the wind It will slow us down,' said Captain Anxious, anxiously stroking his wart. 'Norm, get on the helm and turn us west.'

'Aye aye, captain.' Digby ran for the wheel and spun it to the right.

''Full speed ahead,' the Captain called. 'We'll try and outrun them.' The craft surged forward and heeled in response to his orders but, after a while, it became apparent that the pursuing craft was gaining on them; its image almost filled the glass of the Captain's telescope.

'It's no good Cap'n,' called the mate from his high vantage point. 'They'll be on us in a couple of hours at this rate.'

'We are going to have to make a fight of it. I'll take the helm; you boys break out the cannon.'

'We have a cannon?' Digby asked, surprised. 'Where is it?'

'Cargo bay G,' the Captain replied.

'Oh G for gun, eh?'

'No it's just that bay C was full of cabbages. Now, get the lead out.'

'Where is the powder and shot?' said Ben. 'Bay P or S?'

'The powder is in P, but no shot I'm afraid.'

'No shot? What are we supposed to use for ammunition?' Ben asked Anxious, apprehensively.

'You remember your recipe don't you, get baking.

Prue, you help him.'

'It's a bit late Cap'n, but maybe you better turn windward now. Ye see they can't sail in that direction.'

'No, we'll wait until they close with us, I'll head north, but tell the Sailors to go back to normal speed and save their strength will ye?'

Under Fire

Ben and Captain Ali Anxious stood on the aft deck watching as the Pirate Galley loomed ever closer.

'I don't suppose it is worth parleying, is it?' the Captain asked.

'The Cap'n of the last ship to surrender was set adrift in a long boat five leagues off an island.'

'That sounds reasonable,' said the Captain optimistically. 'Reckon I could row five leagues,'

'Aye, but not without your arms; his were cut off and tied to the stern of the boat to attract the sharks. ahaar.' Ben grimaced

'Aye...' The Captain swallowed hard. 'So we fight. Where's that ammo?'

'Won't be long. Prue is just finishing the icing.'

'Icing!' the Captain exclaimed. 'This is a battle not a tea party!'

'I know Cap'n, but she insisted.'

Norm, Dig and Knobby had rigged the small cannon on a swivel mount in the middle of the foredeck. Casks of gunpowder were stacked behind it and a taper on a long pole was smouldering in Digby's hand as he stood to attention alongside the weapon. Norman had loaded and primed the gun although he was waiting for the first batch of projectiles. He also stood smartly, his ramrod at the ready. They had decided that if they looked professional it might make the pirates think twice.

'Come and get it!' Prudence called from the galley door. Sally and Ben ran down and collected the trays, each covered with a cloth, which they used to hold the hot metal as they carried them to the gun.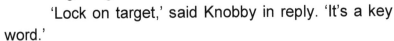

'Ok,' Ben said, 'lock and load'

'Lock what?' said Norman examining the gun.

'Lock on target,' said Knobby in reply. 'It's a key word.'

'These cakes look delicious,' said Digby. He had removed the cloth to reveal the neat rows of pink iced rock cakes.

'I shouldn't try one if you value your teeth,' said Norman. None the less, they both took a tentative bite as they loaded a dozen into the muzzle.

'I saw that Norman Knocker,' came Sally's voice as she returned with another tray. 'Don't try one and put it back, it's unhygienic.'

'But they're...' Norman's protest was interrupted.

'Stand by, I'm turning! As soon as you can, give them a broadside!

'A broadside?' said Digby.

'He means fire the gun,' said Knobby. 'Wait till I give you the nod, then light the fuse.'

The sails of the pirate vessel filled their vision over the stern; there was no need to use the spyglass to read the name on her bow.

'The Black Pig.' Captain Anxious read aloud.

'Aye Cap'n,' said Ben. 'The Scourge of the Eight Seas ahaar.'

'Right... Now,' said the Captain. 'Full speed on port sweeps, steady as ye go starboard.' With Ben relaying his instructions in hoos and eee's to the rowers, he spun the helm and the little ship quickly turned in a tight semicircle.

'Ok boys, let them have it!' the Captain called.

Knobby nodded, Digby lit the fuse and Norman held his ears as the little gun fired issuing a cloud of smoke and pink Icing.

Knobby's aim was true and soon the crew of the Black Pig were rolling about on the deck.

'Reload, reload,' shouted Knobby. 'Let's get another volley in before they recover!' Like a well-oiled team, courtesy of the Captain's bottle, they fired again.

The pirates were still rolling around with laughter at the delicate pink projectiles when the second salvo hit. This one splattered the bridge in blue icing from the second tray of cakes. Norman wanted to maintain the element of surprise.

'Blue now is it ahaar,' Captain Hogwash laughed, 'They be getting serious, ahaar.' However, his laughter turned to concern when he turned to find his helmsman lying on the deck, a blue iced rock cake stuck firmly to his forehead. The wheel was spinning wildly and the sails started to flap ineffectually.

'All hands aloft, trim those sails ye lubbers.' He yelled as he struggled to control the wheel. However, his crew were in further difficulties. Half of them were stuck to the deck by the icing and most of the rest were stuck to them as they tried to help. The decks were too sticky to move about on. Some of the crew had shed their shoes only to have their bare feet stick to the planking.

Back on board the Lexi, the crew were jubilant. Sally was dancing a hornpipe with Ben and the gun crew were cheering and waving their implements. In the excitement, Captain Anxious had forgotten to change course and the little ship continued to turn. It ran under the stern of the bigger vessel and was now coming up the other side.

'Avast there,' he yelled over the din, 'stand by for another broadside.'

'More cakes, more cakes,' yelled Norman as he primed his weapon.

Sally ran to the galley and came back with another tray, green this time.

'That's the last,' she said as she handed them over. They just had time to ram them down the barrel and let fly before they had passed the stricken pirate ships bow. Pink and blue gunge was beginning to ooze out of the bilges as the icing spread.

The Captain allowed the little craft to turn across their bow once again.

'If only we had another batch, we could finish her off,' he muttered. Prudence appeared in the cabin door carrying another hot tray.

'Another batch little lady?' cried Ben 'Hold hard Cap'n and we'll blast them again.'

'No no,' said Pru, 'These are spoilt. I forgot them in the excitement and they got burnt, I was going to throw them over the side.' She pulled back the cloth to reveal a neat baker's dozen of round black objects, wisps of smoke rose from each one.

'Give them here,' Ben roared and grabbed the tray, which he immediately dropped. He stood blowing on his fingers as the burnt offerings at his feet seared their way into the deck. Sally saved the day rushing up with a plate and a pair of tongs she gathered them up and, with a disparaging cry of 'Men!' she sallied forward to the waiting cannon.

Prudence, who insisted on putting butter on his burnt digits, took Ben below.

'These will do the trick,' shouted Norman in excitement, 'better aim for their rigging otherwise you could have someone's eye out with one of these.'

They had started down the starboard side again when Knobby nodded and Digby touched his taper to the fuse. They could see their missiles glow ahead of a trail of smoke as they arced into the sails of the Black Pig.

Captain Ali Anxious gave the order and spun his helm. The rowers pulled together and the Lexi turned to windward leaving the smouldering Captain Hogwash with his smouldering ship and sticky crew in their wake.

Storm Brewing

They kept up a good speed to windward for several hours until they were sure that the Black Pig had not been able to follow. Then they gave the Sailors a break for a swim and something to eat before resuming a southerly course. The sun was low in the western sky when they gathered round the table in the aft cabin for a celebratory meal.

It had taken all that time to get the ship and crew cleaned up. The soot from the cannon washed away easily enough but the spillages from Prue's icing were a different matter. The only known solvent for the sweet sticky substance was saliva. Anything else, even water, just made it gloopier. Prudence, having licked her own fingers, licked Digby clean. Sally licked Norman all over, even where there was no icing, and Knobby set about the spillages on the deck.

'Well,' said Prudence 'any more of that and I will need a bigger oven'

'Perhaps we should lay in a stock of ammunition,' said the Captain, 'It was remarkably effective and I don't think we've seen the last of those scurvy knaves, ahaar. What say ye Ben?'

'Ye'll not be wrong there, Cap'n. Hogwash is a harsh man but he won't keep the respect o' his crew if he is defeated by some townies and covered in pink icing to boot, ahaar.' They all laughed at the memory.

'How be it Knobby?' said the Captain, for once feeling more sea dog than number cruncher, 'do the crows still have them in sight?'

'Aye Captain, I climbed the matht with their food and took a look through the thpyglath. There is thtill some thmoke coming from them but they are definitely in purthuit.' He was having trouble pronouncing his S's 'Is there a thplinter in my tongue?'

'I can't see anything,' said Digby examining the extended pink and blue organ, 'but it is rough enough to scrape the barnacles off the bottom of the Lexi.'

'It's always been capable of that. Perhaps a little oil would help.'

'All right, I take the hint,' said the Captain, 'pass the bottle round Ben'

Ben muttered something about it always being his bottle, took a swig and passed the cod liver oil on. Sally and Prudence declined, preferring a rust tea and orange juice cocktail, commonly known as a Shirley Temple. They tucked into huge cutlets of shark wing which Prudence had sautéed in oil with sauerkraut pasta on the side. Ben liberally grated hard cheese over his dish.

'Those clouds on the horizon look ominous,' he said, almost between mouthfuls. I think we could be in for a storm.' He sprayed oily cheese crumbs onto the table with his last word.

'Ben!' Prudence scolded, 'I think we may have to make you eat with the apes.'

'But what about the smell,' Ben complained.

'They will just have to get used to it,' said Knobby. He and Norm gave each other a high five and they all laughed. 'The old jokes are still the best.'

'With luck, a storm may help us get away but after dinner start baking again and lay that icing on good and thick. Well done everybody.' The Captain raised his mug of tea. They all joined him, clinking their cups together over the table and making more spillages for Prudence to clear up. *Well, it keeps her happy.* Digby thought.

It was another day before the sea started to swell in increasing hillocks of green and white. Unbidden, the Sailors had laid in a supply of kelp, which was left to soak in the bilges. Under Knobby and Ben's supervision, Norm and Dig went around making sure all the hatches were secure and rigged the small staysail to the mast. This gave little propulsion but dampened the roll of the ship sufficiently to keep both sets of sweeps in the water most of the time. The clouds that had hugged the horizon now rolled and boiled above their heads with occasional flashes of lightening illuminating them from time to time. They headed south with the storm building from the east and their pursuers clearly gaining on them from the northwest.

'Avast you young ladies, get below and stay there, ahaar,' said the Captain, 'and make sure there are no loose objects in the galley, ahaar.'

'Aye Aye Capt'n, I just have to finish this batch of ammunition, er . . . aahaaaarr,' said Prudence trying to be seaman-like.

'Why can't I stay on deck and watch the storm Captain Sir?,' asked Sally. She had dressed in a pair of white bell-bottom trousers with a leather waistcoat, a red spotted bandanna covered her hair and she thought she looked quite shipshape. Norman on the other hand thought she looked mostly girl shaped.

'Better get below Sal' he said. 'We don't want you washed overboard, do we?'

'You're not the Captain,' she replied, a fire in her eyes. 'What say ye Cap'n Ali, permission to stay?'

'Permission granted,' said the Captain. He knew better than to argue with a woman of her calibre. 'But first give Prudence a hand to secure the cabin, aye?' Sally stuck her tongue out at Norman and went below. Norman's heart skipped a beat and he knew he loved her.

Digby came staggering up from hold 'O' where he had retrieved a bundle of wet weather clothing. If the storm had not been making such a racket he would no doubt have noticed noises coming from only four bins away as several of the sacks were now quite animated.

He distributed the oilskins as the rain began to fall and, with Sally's return to the deck, they all lashed themselves to something solid. Ben and Captain Anxious were tied to the wheel housing, Digby to the ships rail on the starboard side and Knobby fixed himself to the bow like an inboard figurehead peering ahead for obstructions. Before settling himself, Norman secured Sally to the mast, making sure that she was comfortable but secure. They kissed tenderly before he had to hurry to his station on the port side. He was almost there when, as the ship rolled, a big wave washed across the deck, sweeping him off his feet. Sally screamed as he disappeared from sight.

Man Overboard

Rain lashed the deck like a thousand cat-o-nine-tails; that is nine thousand lashes at a time. The first burst of forked lightening rent the sky, only a short-term rental but enough to illuminate the broiling cauldron of cumulus that seemed as thick as an Uverlander's overcoat.

Digby started to untie himself in order to go after his friend.

'Belay that ye swab,' called the Captain with surprising authority. 'Everyone stay lashed ahaar! There is nothing ye can do against the mighty ocean. As if to prove it, another gigantic wave crashed over them swamping the whole deck. Even Sally, who was unable to undo the love-knot that Norman had tied her with, knew that it was hopeless.

The storm was rampant around them. The sky flashed and crackled with energy, thunder crashed and rumbled both near and far as if a mighty battle was raging for control of the atmosphere. The seas steepened, sometimes they looked up at a mountain of water with foaming tips like snow-caps at the peak, other times they looked down into a valley-like trough, as dark and

deep as the abyss. The little ship rolled and dipped as it was tossed like a toy in the irresistible hands of the elements.

The Sailors, drenched alternately in rain and then in seawater, could do no more than ship their oars and cling to their benches. Helped by Ben, the Captain grimly held onto the wheel and tried to compensate for the roll and prevent the craft from capsizing completely. Digby peered out between sodden eyelids doggedly keeping lookout and trying not to think of his lost friend. Knobby squinted his eyes, keeping watch forward lest they run aground, a fate, as time went on, he almost relished. Sally slumped in her bonds and wept. Great sobs shook her chest. Prudence, unaware of the drama outside, had jammed herself into one of the bolted down chairs and tried to polish a hole in the table.

The storm-ravaged vessel bobbed and weaved, tipped and slipped, climbed and dived all day. There was no let up and, in the darkened sky, no sign of the sun. Eventually the rain stopped and the intervals between the lightning flashes and the rolls of thunder lengthened. The sky cleared from the east and then the darkest blue sky they had ever seen was revealed above. The low clouds to the west were tinged with silver and then golden rays of the setting sun spread across the sky above them. The beautiful sight, however, was completely wasted on Sally who sagged exhausted, both physically and mentally at the mast.

The sea was moderating now and, although they continued to roll about, no waves splashed over onto the decks. Digby released himself and then freed Sally.

He gently guided her towards the cabin wondering how he could break the news to Prudence.

'Help!' a weak but urgent voice called.

Galvanized by a rush of adrenalin, Sally and Dig ran to the rail and looked over the side. There, suspended by the seat of his oilskin trousers, was Norman, stuck fast to the side of the hull by a wayward dribble of Prue's remarkable pink icing.

'The skipper will have my guts for missing that bit,' said Knobby joining them at the rail.

'Well I for one am glad you did,' spluttered Norman. Waves continued to slap into him from time to time. 'Any chance of pulling me up?'

Knobby and Digby reached over, grabbed one of his outstretched arms each and heaved. Norman wriggled his feet out of his boots to release them and the bedraggled body was lifted clear out of the firmly stuck leggings. He was soon laid out on the deck, his two friends on their knees beside him panting for breath.

'Don't you ever do that to me again, Norman Knocker,' Sally scolded and then flinging herself astride him, she pinched his nose and firmly adhered her lips to his open mouth.

'Tea anyone?' said Prudence from the cabin doorway.

Gone South

The Sailors consumed the last of the kelp stored in the bilge and, at the same time, they bailed out the excess water that had accumulated during the storm. Hooing and eeeing in a cheerful way they returned to their task of rowing the craft ever further south.

Before joining the others at supper, Knobby scaled the mast and scanned the horizon. There was no sign of the pirate ship in any direction and clear skies prevailed to the south and east. He also coaxed the crows out from hiding with a little stale bread and set them to watch.

The crew celebrated their survival with a sumptuous meal eaten with respectful care off the gleaming, if somewhat thinner, cabin table. Even Ben refrained from speaking with his mouth full, allowing the inherent overflow from his lips to drop into his lap instead.

'We are set fair to continue our voyage me hearties,' said Captain Ali, 'but before all the excitement I was looking over the books and have to warn ye that we do not have the supplies to complete the trip as planned. With the three extra crewmembers, and an unexpected consumption of flour and sugar to make ammunition, we must find a port in which to replenish our provision, ahaar. What say ye, should we turn back now or go on into uncharted territory?'

'If we turn back now we may well run into Hogwash and his crew again,' said Ben. 'I doubt we will be so lucky next time.'

'Let him try if he must,' said Sally, 'we whipped him once and we can do it again.'

The others cheered agreement with an enthusiasm none of them actually felt. Digby, fondling the wart on the right side of his face, brought a level of sobriety to the proceedings.

'If we turn back now our quest will be lost. We will be laughing stocks when we arrive home. Norm and I will have wasted our college fund for nothing. We must go on.'

'Dig is right,' said Norman. 'I, for one, feel we must go on. There must be land to the south, what about Uverland?' there was a sharp intake of breath from all around the table.

'The land of dark foreboding,' Prudence whispered on behalf of them all.

'What say ye Ben?' asked the Captain. 'Ye've sailed these parts more than most. Is there a friendly port to the south where we can restock the ship?'

'Well,' said the old sea dog, stroking his own wart in contemplation, 'there is an island frequented by pirates and merchantmen alike, aye but it would be hard to find, ahaar.'

'P, p, pirates, again,' said Prudence. 'I don't think I could handle more pirates. I'm running out of things to clean.'

'Now don't take on so, young Miss Prudence, this is a free port. No one would dare cause trouble there for fear of breaking the seaman's code to say nothing of upsetting the Governor.'

'Upsetting the Governor?' said Digby.

'I said; say nothing of upsetting the Governor!' said Ben with a laugh, 'but to be serious, Governor Piper can be a formidable man, ahaar. He is a former scourge of the high seas, aye, and renowned slaughterer of the lower tonic ranges. When we arrive we will be forced to endure one of his operatic recitals and karaoke nights. This is an experience far worse than any torture that one might receive from Captain Hogwash, although marginally less fatal, ahaar.'

'Two questions,' said Captain Ali, 'One - will we be able to buy provisions there? and two - can we find this island?'

'There is no doubt you can buy provisions if you have the gold, but to find it is a different matter, aye. Do ye know our exact position Cap'n? ahaar.'

'Not exactly,' said the Captain stroking his wart. 'We drifted all over the place in that storm and I can't rely on the time now what with the sun disappearing from time to time, and all . . . er . . . ahaar.'

'Aye well, that's the rub ye see. The island lies close to the waterfall at the end of the world and the current rushes past it at a terrible rate of knots. If we miss we might be carried right over the abyss.'

'If the current is so strong,' said Prudence, 'why doesn't the island get carried away? Surely even hundreds of apes can't row an island that hard forever.'

'Aye, now don't you worry about that young miss,' said Ben. 'This is not a floating island, it is a giant peak of rock sticking out of the ocean floor, so it can never wash away, ahaar.'

'How strange,' said Digby. 'An island that doesn't move, this I must see.' He stroked his left wart vigorously.

'I still have two questions,' said the Captain. 'One - can we find it? and two - do we want to risk it?'

'I for one would love to go,' said Norman, 'but I cannot risk my lovely Sally's life so I say we turn back now.'

'You speak for yourself Norman Knocker,' squealed Sally. 'I vote we go on!'

'If Sally is game to go so am I,' said Prudence.

'And I,' said Digby. 'What about you Knobby?'

'Never say die,' said Knobby with a shrug.

'Ahaar, I suppose that settles it,' said the Captain, 'provided we can find it. I will look at my charts.'

'They won't do ye any good, Cap'n,' said Ben, 'but I have a chart in my locker, ahaar. I'll fetch it, aye.' And with that, he went below.

Passing storage bin 'E' he slid and nearly fell over on the deck that had become slippery between there and bay 'C' but rushed onto his locker. I'll tell young Knobby to clean that mess up, he thought as he hurried back but by the time he reached the cabin, it had gone right out of his head.

'There it is,' he said, having spread the chart out. 'The island of Ever-Rest.'

They gathered round and studied the map, each holding down one side to stop it rolling up, while the

Captain took up his callipers and measured the position of the island.

'It's only a week's sail from the coast of Uverland,'

'The land of dark . . .' the others chanted.

'Yes, yes and all that,' interrupted the Captain, 'and also a week's sail to the edge of the world,' he went on.

'Less,' said Ben, 'the current in them parts will pull you that distance in only three days, ahaar.'

'The problem is, where are we now?' said the Captain. 'How far east have we come and how far south must we go?'

'The apes may be able to help there,' said Ben. 'They seem to have an instinct about these things. Let's go on deck and ask Phd.'

The Captain and Ben rolled up the chart and left to consult the senior Sailor leaving Digby to help Prudence with the washing up.'

'Would you really have given everything up to save me from danger?' said Sally in Norman's ear as they left for their cabin. Their giggles could still be heard some time later.

Land Ho

Phd had confidently pointed to the south east when she had been shown the chart. So they sailed in that direction for a week. Sometimes in sunshine and sometimes in rain they pursued the same course. The further south they went the longer the nights became and as a consequence the shorter the days.

In the middle of one long night when Knobby was about to change over with Ben, he climbed the mast for a last look round. A thin coating of cloud obscured the stars as he strolled round the roof of the crow's nest, swinging from the masthead by one hand. He almost lost his footing as his gaze alighted on the distant eastern horizon. The clouds, clustered low to the sea, seemed to glow red as if lit by a distant fire. Fascinated he watched the phenomenon as the glow increased until Ben came on deck.

'Ahoy Ben, up here,' he called, 'I see a glow to the east. Would that be from Ever-Rest?'

Ben clambered up the rigging to join the mate and clinging one each side of the swaying masthead he stared at the glow which by now was beginning to wane.

'No matey,' said Ben once he had his breath back, 'that be the southern sun ahaar.'

During the next two weeks the glow increased each night until the huge red orb of the southern sun rose clear of the horizon. By the same token, their familiar golden orb rose less high and for less time each day until they both shared equal time in ascendancy. The day was now divided into equal quarters which they called Red Day followed by Red Night then Gold Day and Gold Night. This made it very difficult to tell the time by the mast's shadow so they had to rely on the ships clock which had stopped several times on the journey, mostly due to the Captain forgetting to wind it.

It was at this point that Phd clambered up to the wheelhouse and, with hoo's and eee's, indicated to Ben that they should now turn to the east. A few days later they came across a small floating island. It was drifting steadily in the same direction as they were. As luck would have it, it appeared on the horizon during the middle of a Gold Day and the crow's agitated cries brought it to their attention. During the Red Days the birds refused to leave their nest, remaining with their heads under their wings until a more familiar daylight returned.

The Sailors became excited too as they caught scent of the vegetation and, as they drew alongside, they stopped rowing and lined the rail to get a better look. To their disappointment the burgh was devoid of life, just a floating chunk of dead weed. They soon returned to their steady rowing, leaving the island to follow in their wake.

Over the next few days they passed several more veggie-burgs; all of them were in the same condition and seemed to follow the same course. It was the persistent breeze from the east that made them realise that their speed had picked up. When the Sailors went over the side for their daily forage they were swept forward in the strong current and had to swim quite hard to get back. The breeze slackened when they were not under oar power but it slowed the vessel enough to make quite a difference.

'We are getting close now Cap'n,' said Ben. 'Best rest the Sailors and keep a good watch until we sight it.'

It was a clear night when Ever-Rest first came into view. Sally, who loved to stand atop the mast, was the first to spot it. A bright light shone from the top of what might have been any of the dozens of floating islands that dotted the sea around them. Gradually the light rose higher as they closed with it until a dark conical mass started to reveal itself below.

'Land Ho!' she called to Norman who was patrolling the deck below, as he always did, when she was aloft.

'Where away?' he called back, surprising himself at his seaman-like response.

'Three points off the larboard bow,' she called back.

'Where?' said Norman.

'Oh, over there, you lummox,' she replied pointing. 'I see a light.'

Captain Anxious ran on deck wearing his nightshirt and carrying his telescope. Ben arrived close behind, stumbling as he tried to negotiate the companionway whilst pulling on his trousers at the same time. He careened into the back of the Captain and the pair tumbled in a flurry of arms and legs across the deck. Knobby, who had appeared from nowhere, managed to catch the telescope before it rolled over the side. Leaving the semi naked officers to sort themselves out he sprang to the foredeck and put the glass to his eye.

'I see it,' he yelled in excitement. 'We will be there by dawn!'

Western Approaches

The adventurers gathered on the deck just before dawn to watch the amazing sight. The island of Ever-Rest rose out of the sea a few miles in front and to one side

of them. The sea, for its part, underlined the land mass with white foam from the waves breaking on its steep shores. The peaks of three mountains stood proud, tall and barren above the lush green of the lower valleys and the steep coastal cliffs.

'See how fast the current is,' said Captain Anxious, favouring his wart. As if to demonstrate the point, one of the many floating masses of weed that accompanied them on their approach rolled into the static land mass only to be smashed into a thousand pieces on the rocks. The debris was swept away around the side of the island in no time flat.

'That is what will happen to us if we attempt a landing there.' The Captain went on.

'Aye, Cap'n. The approach has to be made from the east in the shelter of the island where there is slack water, ahaar.' Ben was standing on the wheelhouse roof for a better view. 'Look ye there Cap'n, a ship is about to make its approach.'

To the east, a craft of similar size to The Lexi was moving under full sail across the line of the current. It appeared to be heading directly at the side of the island.

'I hope they are not pirates,' said Prudence polishing the ships wheel with her apron. 'I'm out of flour.'

'Now don't ye worry Miss Prudence,' said Ben. 'They won't start any trouble in these waters.'

'They look like they will run aground.' Digby climbed up to join Ben on the roof. It did indeed look like the sailing craft was about to crash headlong into the steep, rocky face of the mountainous land mass. Captain Anxious was about to order full speed in order to overhaul the other craft and at least pick up survivors when under the influence of the strong current when it was carried past the eastern end and started to disappear behind the Island.

'That is what we must do, aye,' said Ben, "cos if we miss the slack water our Sailors will never be able to row us back against that current, ahaar.' He looked at Phd who had joined them on deck. She hoo'd once, shrugged and ambled back to her place in the rowing deck. A couple of hoo's and eee's from her once she was sat comfortably and they began to row. Captain Anxious took the helm with Digby alongside him, Knobby climbed the mast and woke the crows then, as they swirled around him in panic, took up his position as lookout.

They could hear the waves breaking now like distant thunder growing steadily in volume. The spray was carried on the strong breeze to sting their eyes as they peered towards the looming mountain ahead of them.

'Come on Sal,' said Norman, 'let's go forward and keep watch from there.'

'I think my stove needs cleaning,' said Prudence. 'Let me know when we are there.' She disappeared below to find her brush and black lead.

'A little more speed if you please, Mr Bun,' said the Captain. Ben, from his position on the wheelhouse roof, relayed the instruction to the rowers who increased their pace.

'It's all about timing,' said the Captain to Digby, 'Give me a hand with the wheel, she keeps trying to turn into the current.'

In the bow, Sally and Norm leaned over the rail. Below them the sea was deep and dark. Sally's eyes sparkled with excitement but Norman's could not deny his trepidation as the cliff face filled their view.

'Steady as she goes, number one,' said the Captain, the calm of his voice belying the turmoil in his stomach.

'Aye Aye Cap'n,' said Ben,

'Give us two more points to port,' the Captain said to Digby.

'What?' said Digby, clutching the wheel tight enough to whiten his knuckles.

'Left hand down a bit,' said the Captain.

'We're getting awfully close,' yelled Norman from the bow. The waves breaking on the rugged rock face were splashing back, soaking them from head to foot. Sally grinned and said nothing.

'One hundred metres,' Knobby called from the crow's nest, his voice nearly lost in the roar from the pounding waves.

'Ease the oars,' the Captain commanded. 'Another two points if you please Mr Dingle.'

As the craft swung to follow the current, Captain Ali ran to the starboard side, the cliff face was only metres away, the sea in between boiled and frothed. 'Another point Mr Dingle,'

Digby fought the wheel but had no breath to sound the aye aye Sir his mouth formed.

'Another point, ye lubber.' The Captain was anxious. Ben leapt down to give Digby a hand. The wall of rock seemed to lean out over them as it slid rapidly by. It looked like they would just make it. Their bow pushed out beyond the end of the rock wall and Norman could see the area of calm water tapering away from the sheltered shore.

An oar struck the rocks, throwing the ape that was handling it onto his back. Another struck, then another causing chaos among the starboard bank of rowers. The craft twisted out of control as the current swept them past the point of land. Phd eee'd and hoo'd at her team in an attempt to sort out the confusion. In the meantime, they were being swept further away from the slack water. The efforts of the port sweeps turned the craft in a pirouette as the swirling current buffeted the rudder beyond the combined strengths of Ben and Dig. They fell to the floor as the wheel swung to its stops first one way, then the other.

Somehow, the Sailors got themselves sorted out and. under Phd's direction, they righted the course. Between them, the three Urlanders at the helm managed to regain control of the wheel. They had drifted a long way down stream. The area of slack water had reduced to a narrow point some distance off the port bow. Following Knobby's directions, pointing from his vantage point above, they headed for it, the Sailors pulling on their sweeps for all that they were worth. Failure would herald only one result - a trip over the waterfall at the edge of the world and oblivion.

Safe Haven

Heroic efforts by Phd and her stalwart rowers gradually overcame the strong current and they managed to catch the tail of the slack water. Here the sea eddied and rolled in confusion as the conflicting influences struggled for dominance. The exhausted apes still had to pull hard to keep them from being spilled out into the main stream again. Captain Ali took the wheel on his own in order to respond to the sudden vagaries of the turmoil under their keel, calling on Ben occasionally to add some power to the steering.

Digby went below to see how Prudence had fared. The galley stove gleamed black and shiny and alongside it stood Prudence, equally black but by no means shiny.

'Is it all over?' she asked. Her white teeth flashed a brilliant smile amid her darkened face.

'We're past the worst,' Digby said. 'Have you been having fun?'

'Yes, great fun,' she replied. 'Time for tea then.' She picked up the teapot from the dresser depositing a black smear on its white handle. 'I think I had better wash my hands first,' she said.

'And that's not the only thing!' Digby laughed and hugged her covering his own clothes in black lead polish.

Up on the bow Norman and Sally were also hugging each other in congratulation; this was quite an extended process involving an inordinate amount of kissing as well.

At last, the Lexi was free of the turbulent area and, although a little gentle rowing was required to keep them heading in the right direction, the Sailors were able to rest a little.

'That was a close run thing,' said the Captain as Knobby joined him at the wheel. 'I think we owe the rowers a serious scratching, don't you?'

'We certainly do Captain,' said Knobby, 'I'll get started.'

'I'll give ye a hand, Mr mate,' said Ben as they collected their back scratchers. Norman and Sally joined in and soon the apes were revelling in their attention four by four.

'Tea is up,' said the newly scrubbed Sally as she brought a tray loaded with cups and a plate of scones up to the bridge. For the first time they were able to contemplate the sight of the port of Ever-Rest.

They were still some miles off the coast but ahead of them they could see a deep fjord, the sides sheer slabs of dull grey granite. At its end, sparkling like a diamond against a surrounding blanket of deepest green, was the port. The little craft that had preceded them, its sails furled, sat at anchor just off the harbour wall. Beyond this, dozens of masts could be made out against the whitewashed walls of the warehouses that lined the docks.

'What's the protocol here, Mr Bun?' asked the Captain as he passed his bottle of oil round the company to fortify the rust tea.

'Anchor up and wait for the pilot cutter,' said Ben, spraying the company with crumbs. 'Sorry Pru,' he spluttered as he cleaned up the mess.

'I'm getting used to it,' she said with a shrug.

'There will of course be a fee, ahaar.' Ben went on this time with an empty mouth.

'Do ye know the amount?' Digby asked, stroking his right wart.

'Negotiable,' said Ben.

'And if we can't agree?' asked the Captain.

'They sink ye, ahaar,' said Ben.

They were entering the mouth of the fjord by now and, high on each side, the ominous sight of battlements with cannons run out could be determined.

'We could leave now I suppose,' said the Captain then, stroking his wart, 'How much could they charge? I'm sure they will be most reasonable.'

By the time they reached the outer harbour, the small sailing craft was being towed into its berth by a longboat. This was powered by eight rowers, not apes as they would have expected, but people.

'They don't have Sailors here,' Ben said in response to the Captain's puzzled look.

'Will ours be alright?' Digby was worried for his furry companions who had endeared themselves to all the crew.

'Don't worry young Sir,' said Ben, 'others have been here before and moved on. It is just that they do not have much of a resident population this far south.'

'So they have to do their own rowing?' said Norm.

'In a way,' Ben replied. 'Mostly the rowers be criminals condemned to spend their life in service of the Governor, ahaar.'

'W... what kind of criminals? p, p, p, pirates?' Prudence stammered.

'Don't you worry my dear,' Ben reassured her. 'Any pirates will be on their best behaviour here. Governor Piper does not concern himself with any acts outside the island or the slack water zone, ahaar. These criminals be only thieves, murderers, or those who did not appreciate his singing.'

'All hands stand by to drop anchor,' the Captain called interrupting their cheery conversation.

As soon as the Lexi came to a stop, the Sailors swarmed over the side for a wash and to forage for food. Captain Ali left Knobby with the task of making everything ship-shape on deck and disappeared below. Prudence set about polishing the compass binnacle with gusto, while Sally climbed the mast to feed the crows and get a better view. Norman paced the deck below as usual.

'When was the last time you were here?' Digby asked Ben as they leaned on the rail and watched the sun dip behind the bulk of the distant mountain.

'Oh, that will be about eleven years ago, ahaar. Just afore I fell out with Cap'n Argent. We called in here to make a deposit in the bank, ahaar.'

'The bank?' said Digby with surprise, 'I thought pirates buried their treasure.'

'Aye they used to but nowadays they mostly put it on deposit here. Y'see too much treasure was getting lost by falling through the bottoms of the floating islands so Governor Piper licensed an old sea dog by the name of Lloyd to arrange suitable internment here.' Ben pointed towards the docks. 'Ye see that tall building yonder? That be his vault, aye.'

'You mean that great big building is full of treasure?'

'Bless ye heart no, that just houses the treasure maps. The treasures are buried out in the jungle all over the island, ahaar'

The town was falling into shadow now; lights were coming on here and there as the lamplighters did their rounds. The crows ceased their excited circling of the mast and returned to their nest to sleep.

'Isn't it time you came down now Sal,' Norm called.

'It's so beautiful,' replied his girlfriend. 'Please come up and watch the sunset with me.'

'I, I'd rather not Sal. Come down so that we can watch it from here.' Norman had never been happy with heights.

'Wuss,' she called back, but started to descend. She had one hand gripping the edge of the top platform when a large owl landed on it. Arriving out of the gloom on silent wings it took her completely by surprise. Losing her grip, she tumbled backwards, arms and legs flailing as she plummeted towards the deck. One foot thrust through the shrouds becoming entangled in their lattice of rope work and arresting her fall with a jolt, leaving her hanging upside down in mid-air.

Norman was up the rigging like a monkey up a coconut palm.

'Are you alright?' he asked between pants for breath.

'Do I look alright?' she replied. Her hair had come loose and cascaded down, fluttering in the gentle breeze.

'You never looked lovelier,'

'Are you going to get me down or not?' she demanded. Knobby arrived carrying a length of rope over his shoulder and together they looped it under her arms and, passing it over a nearby bracket on the mast, dropped the end to the deck. With Digby and Ben taking the strain, Norman released her trapped foot and they lowered her gently down. Norman was there in time to gather her up in his arms before her feet touched the deck.

'Any bones broken?' asked Digby.

'No I'm fine, really I am,' Sally said. 'You can put me down now Norm.'

'No I think I had better carry you straight to bed.' Norman looked determined.

'Sounds like a plan,' said Sally with a smile. She kissed him hard on the lips as he made his way towards the cabin.

Knobby had continued up the mast to investigate the intruder. The owl sat calmly waiting, its large round eyes blinked directly at him as he popped his head over the top of the barrel.

'It has a message attached to its leg,' he called back to those below. No sooner had he detached the paper from the impassive bird than it took off and with a single silent flap glided off towards the town. The creature was silhouetted for a moment against the dying rays of the setting sun until it dipped and merged into the darker background.

The Captain was sound asleep in his cabin so Knobby handed the message to Digby. With the other two peering over his shoulder, Digby held the paper up to catch the last remaining light and read it out loud.

Boarding Party.

The message was on fancy crested notepaper and written in a precise and pedantic hand. Digby read it out to his two colleagues.

'"On behalf of His Excellency Peter Piper the Third, I bid you welcome,"' he recited, 'We regret that we are unable to accommodate you with a berth in the harbour tonight due to the lateness of the hour, and my wife will have my dinner ready. We must request that you remain at anchor until the morning whereupon I will attend on you to complete the necessary formalities. Would you be so kind as to set an anchor light and remain where you are until then. Thank you for your cooperation. Please note that failure to comply will result in being blown out of the water."' Digby looked up at the cannons on the fjord walls above and gulped. 'It is signed with a squiggle I can't make out, then "Harbour-master, Port of Ever-Rest."'

'I don't think we've got an anchor light,' said Knobby looking at the coil of chain on the deck.

'Fetch ye an oil lamp from the cabin and haul 'er up the mast,' said Ben. 'That will do, ahaar. I'm off to me hammock,'

Digby helped Knobby set the lamp and then settled himself down in the wheelhouse where Prudence had fallen asleep propped up against the gleaming brass compass binnacle. Knobby climbed the mast to keep watch, hoping that the cool fresh breeze would keep him awake for the three hours until dawn.

***

'All hands on deck, Pilot Cutter approaching,' the Captain roared. He stood at the rail with his telescope focused on the small craft which had appeared from behind the harbour wall. The southern sun had heaved a third of its bulk above the horizon and its ruddy glow made the flat calm waters of the fjord look like a pool of blood. The rowing boat was making good speed towards them, a small pink wave delineated its bow and little tufts of pink spray flashed off the tips of the eight oars as they broke the surface.

In the bow, the official struck a determined pose. With one foot up on the gunwale, he stared ahead, one hand on his raised knee, the other gripping a clipboard which he had tucked under his arm like a sergeant majors baton. He was wearing a crisp white suit which, in the dawn light, was rendered a rather pretty shade of pink, as were the plumes in this red tricorn hat. His black knee length boots were trimmed with two bands of gold braid to match those on his cuffs and the large shaggy epaulets that adorned his shoulders.

'Stand by to receive a pompous little twit, ahaar,' Ben said as he joined the Captain at the rail.

'I am sure he will turn out to be a perfectly pleasant chap,' replied Captain Ali, stroking his wart. He handed over his telescope for his second in command to take a better look.

'Ahaar, just as I thought, a bumptious jumped up pen pusher if ever I saw one.' Ben handed the telescope to Digby as he appeared from the wheelhouse. 'Look ye there, ahaar.'

'Wow, nice outfit,' said Digby in admiration.

'No good land lubber,' Ben muttered, 'I'm going to find a piece of cheese.'

'We ran out of cheese two days ago,' said Prudence as she made her way down to the galley, 'all we have left is sprouts and a few sacks of cabbages.'

'Well I'm going to look in the hold anyway,' said Ben, for once in a bad mood.

'Good,' said the Captain, 'and stay there until this...this...'

'Twit,' suggested Digby.

'Officer,' corrected the Captain. 'Whatever he is, I don't want to send him back with his nice uniform sprayed with cheese crumbs, ahaar.'

'No chance of that,' complained Ben as he went below.

'Knobby, stand by to pipe our visitors aboard,' Captain Ali called to the mate. Knobby was already prepared. He rolled out a rope ladder over the side and stood bleary eyed, but at attention, at its head.

Harbour Dues.

The Captain sat behind his desk resplendent in his number two uniform. This was every bit as grand as his number one but somewhat frayed about the edges and, although freshly laundered, more ingrained with food stains. As the harbourmaster entered, Ali stood and bowed so low his wart brushed the table in front of him.

'Captain Ali Anxious, I presume,' the official ignored the bow and the outstretched hand that followed it.

'At your service Sir,' the Captain replied.

'Reason for your visit?'

'Er . . . would you like some tea?'

'Reason for visit?'

'To purchase supplies.'

'Nature of voyage?' The official did not look up from the clipboard as he ticked the boxes in his form with a large quill pen.

'Exploration,' said the Captain. 'Are you sure you won't have some tea . . . or some cod liver oil perhaps?'

'Cod liver oil,' the man looked up at last, 'you have a quantity?'

'A limited amount, but you are very welcome to join me in a dram.'

'It is my duty,' the harbourmaster cleared his throat, 'to examine all such contraband for quality, kindly pour me a sample.'

'That would be a pleasure Sir.' Captain Ali turned to the cupboard behind him and collected one of his two remaining bottles and two glasses.

'Length of vessel?' the official returned to his form but now kept one eye on the glass as the Captain filled it.

'Twenty metres,' said the Captain as he filled the glasses to the brim.

'And how long do you intend to stay?'

'Just long enough to re-provision for our trip and maybe do a little sightseeing in this wonderful city of yours. About three days should be sufficient.'

'Two weeks,' said the official, eyeing the glass that the Captain slid towards him.

'Oh I don't think . . .'

'All visitors are required to attend at least one of his Excellency's concerts; the next one is in ten days' time.' He raised the glass and sniffed the contents.

'Oh, I see . . . Your very good health.' The Captain raised the glass to his lips. The two men took a hefty draught of the thick liquid.

'Best put us down for ten days then.'

'You will need a couple of days for your ears to recover,' said the official with, at last, the semblance of a smile. Captain Ali topped up his guest's tumbler.

'Really,' he said, 'that good aye.'

The official spluttered into his glass suppressing a laugh. 'You might say that,' he said as a dribble of oil made its way down towards the small wart on the left side of his chin. He wiped it with his finger and then rubbed it into the protuberance. 'Ahem . . .' he returned to his clipboard. 'Number of crew?'

'Seven Urlanders and eight Sailors,' said the Captain. 'Would you care for a bite to eat?'

'Sailors?' queried the harbourmaster.

'Yes, you know, the rowers'

'Oh the animals, they count as livestock. Eight you say?'

'Er . . . yes . . . eight.'

'Cargo?'

'None.' said the Captain. 'The holds are bare except for a few bags of sprouts and cabbages; would you care to inspect?'

'Inspect your sprouts, yuk, I think not.' The inspector downed the last of his drink and placed the glass back on the table next to the almost empty bottle.

'Now let me see,' he started to write his calculations on the back of the form, glancing up at his glass from time to time.

'Twenty-four metres times twenty-eight days as one shilling a day, that's . . .'

'Er, that's twenty metres for fourteen days,' the Captain corrected.

'There are fourteen red days and fourteen yellow days in a fortnight.'

'Oh I see, but . . .'

'You Captains always underestimate the size of your vessel. However, we could measure it.'

'Perhaps we should,' said the Captain.

'Measuring fee is one hundred shillings,' the official smiled as he added the figure to the bill.

'Oh, I wouldn't want to put you to any trouble,' said the Captain. He drained the remains of the bottle into the official's glass.

The harbourmaster grunted, scratched two lines through the last entry and perused the half-full tumbler. The Captain produced the second and last bottle from his cupboard and topped the glass up.

'Twenty metres, by twenty-eight days, that's five hundred and sixty shillings, plus eight for the animals and seventy for the crew. Harbour fees six hundred and thirty-eight plus VAT.

'What's VAT?'

'Vagrant added tax. If a vessel has no cargo, it is considered to be without assets, thereby a vagrant. Ten percent. Let's call it seven hundred and ten shall we?'

'Let's not' said the Captain, 'I have sprouts in the hold; they are cargo.' He pushed the nearly full bottle in the official's direction.

'They are provisions,' said the official, making room in his glass with a big swig.

'Would you eat them?'

'I see your point. Ok, call it six fifty then.'

'Done,' said the Captain. 'Have a drink.' They both stood, the official a little unsteadily and, in a surprising feat of coordination, clinked their glasses together.

'Just one small matter,' said the official as he slumped back in his chair.

'And that is?' the Captain had turned and was already unlocking his chest where he kept his coins.

'The little matter of smuggling.'

'Smuggling? Smuggling what?'

'Cod liver oil.' The official grinned; his bleary eyes were becoming bloodshot. One hundred shillings, minimum fine.'

'But I only have one bottle left and it is for medicinal purposes.'

'Medical purposes, what medical purposes?'

'Well you are looking well on it!'

'But I won't be when it wears off,' was the regretful reply.

'Perhaps you had better take this last bottle with you for later then,' said the Captain.

'A good idea, Ali old pal, a good idea.' The official tucked the bottle away in the pocket of his oil stained white jacket and stood to leave. 'Give the harbour fees to my attendant and we will say no more about it.' He wobbled towards the door. Captain Ali took seven bags of coins from his chest, counted out fifty from one and retied it.

The official stood blinking in the red daylight, his cocked hat perched on the back of his head. He swayed back and forth even though there was no movement in the deck below him.

Captain Anxious joined the deck party and handed the moneybags to one of the attendants. The giant henchman, with an efficiency that belied his dumb appearance, weighed each bag in his hands and wrote out a receipt for the exact amount. The other attendant gathered up the harbourmaster, throwing him over his shoulder. Catching the dislodged hat behind his back with his free hand, he marched towards the ladder. The whole thing was accomplished with a military precision as if part of a standard routine.

'Would you like us to tow you into your berth, Captain Sir, or will you follow us under your own power,' said the attendant with the coins.

'Under our own power I think,' said the Captain. Before they clambered over the side, Captain Ali slipped a shilling coin into each of the henchmen's hands.

The two giants beamed their gratitude and re-joined their waiting craft. Propping the snoring Harbourmaster in the bow, they took up their positions standing to attention and the longboat eased away.

'Ready with the oars!' called the Captain as he made his way to the wheelhouse, 'we have to follow the pompous little twit into harbour.'

Into Harbour.

Knobby took up his position in the crow's nest to keep an eye on the departing pilot boat while the others winched up the anchor. The apes got into their stride with a level of enthusiasm that took Captain Ali by surprise and he had to get Ben to calm them down before they overran the smaller vessel. With Ben at his side he took the wheel leaving Digby, Norman and the girls, once the anchor was stowed away, to stand on the foredeck and admire the city as they approached it. The red sun was past its azimuth by now and the buildings shone pink, white or purple, depending on their aspect.

'It's so pretty,' said Prudence. 'It looks like a giant wedding cake.'

'Don't give them ideas,' murmured Digby in her ear, 'they're embarrassing enough already.' They glanced at the other couple who were cuddling close together, their eyes torn between the vista in front of them and each other's.

'Ah, but it is so sweet.' replied Prudence. 'Don't you find it romantic?'

'I suppose.' In fact he did, more than his left wart cared to admit. His right one however wanted him to declare his love for Prudence to the whole world, flat, round or whatever shape it was.

They glided past the harbour entrance with its beacon fires like giant torches mounted on the end of the walls. Inside was a jumble of ships in all shapes and sizes, all carried masts hung with loosely furled sails in a variety of colours. A couple of small sailing craft tacked back and forth in the open space between the moorings. A variety of small rowing boats vied between the warehouse jetties and some larger vessels that were anchored in the deep water at the middle of the harbour. Along the outer wall fishing boats were drawn up, the powerful odour of fish guts and seaweed made Digby feel quite hungry. The rowers had eased their oars now and the Lexi slid forward by momentum alone. After the peace of the fjord, the noise that carried from the harbour side was loud and, depending on the bias of your wart, either daunting or exciting. Digby was of course undecided about it. Prudence took to polishing the ship's rail with the hem of her apron. Sally wriggled and jiggled in Norman's arms, an action which completely took his mind away from the prospect of landfall.

'The pilot wants us to put in over there,' Knobby called from crow's-nest. He pointed away to the right. The last remaining free space along the landward wall was almost exactly the length of their craft. With the Captain's skilful hand on the wheel, and considerable intuitive action by the Sailors on the oars, the Urlander's ship entered its berth with consummate ease. On the quayside a small crowd had gathered to watch the arrival of the strange sail-less craft. Disappointed that there were no dramas, many of them drifted away while others, eager to satisfy their curiosity, gathered closer to peer at the crew. There was no shortage of hands to take their mooring lines and tie them to the davits set on the harbour wall. An argument broke out between two men over how the bowline should be tied resulting in the pair of them falling in the water. Knobby, who had scuttled down from the crows-nest, leapt ashore, finished securing the rope and ran back to make sure that the stern line was secured to his satisfaction. The crowd recoiled from his passing, no doubt out of respect for his position, or possibly due to the fact that, as water on board had been strictly rationed for the last two weeks, he had nobly given up washing. The throng resumed their position as soon as the mate returned on board, craning their collective necks to get a view of the other occupants.

'Avast there,' said the Captain, 'afore ye rush ashore we need to clean and tidy the ship.'

'And ourselves,' said Prudence, sniffing her armpit.

'Do we niff a bit then?' Digby said, making similar investigation of his own underarm. 'I hadn't noticed.'

'The land lubbers will,' said Ben, 'Er . . . Cap'n Sir, would it be ok to dismiss the Sailors. They be anxious to get ashore and explore yon jungle for relatives, ahaar.'

'How will we get them back should we need to leave?' the Captain asked, surveying the distant tree tops at the edge of town.

'Don't worry, Cap'n, ahaar, I have a recall whistle.' He pulled a silver cylinder out of his pocket. 'They can hear it over great distances, ahaar.' He put it to his lips and gave it the briefest of puffs. Despite no sound being heard by the Urlanders, Phd leapt on deck and grabbed the device from him.

'Eee, eee, eee,' she admonished him in no uncertain terms before thrusting the whistle into Digby's hands. 'Hoo hoo, eee,' she instructed.

'Only when you need them and never when they are in sight,' Ben translated. The crowd on the dockside had recoiled at the sudden appearance of the two and a half metre green furred monster. They scattered in all directions when all eight of the creatures swarmed over the side and, forming up into two neat rows, set off at an ambling trot towards the edge of town.

Left in peace, the Urlanders soon had the vessel shipshape and squandered the last of the ships fresh water to take a long-awaited bath. Dressed in clean clothes they assembled on deck looking pink and shiny in the dying rays of the setting southern sun ready to explore the port and find a restaurant with enough cheese to satisfy Ben's undiminished craving.

Café Society

In party mood, the intrepid crew of the Lexi ran out the gangplank and descended to dry land at last. Prudence clung to Digby's arm as the ground felt like it was moving under her feet. Norman was struck by the same phenomenon and clung to Sally.

'I thought this was a fixed island,' said Digby to the Captain. 'I think I need another shot of your sea sickness medicine.' He had started to green up again.

'Can't help I'm afraid. That lily livered port official took the last of my stash.' Captain Ali's face was a picture of regret.

'Your body has got used to the roll of the ship, young Sir,' said Ben. 'The feeling will soon pass as you get your shore legs back, ahaar.' He set off along the quay with a pronounced seaman's gait which they all found themselves adopting as they followed.

At the end of the quay was a large gate guarded by the two henchmen from the pilot boat. Alongside it was a small office containing the small port official.

'I will see if I can arrange a delivery of water for the ship,' said Captain Ali, ducking inside the small door. For want of space inside the others watched through the window as the captain entered into negotiations once again.

'Good evening, Sir,' the Captain began. 'I regret I didn't catch your name on our previous encounter.'

'Squiggle,' said the official. 'Harbour Master Simon Squiggle at your service.'

'So pleased to make your acquaintance, er . . . Simon, may I call you Simon?'

'No.' It was clear that the effects of the afternoon oiling had worn off. 'Not on duty. Have you come to pay your landing fees?'

'What landing fees? We paid our dues out in the harbour.' The Captain bristled.

'Ah, but you have come ashore now. Seven shillings.'

Captain Anxious rummaged in his purse and found the requisite sum and slammed it down on the small desk. 'Anything else?' he growled.

'Just one small thing,' Harbour Master Squiggle smiled as he scooped the coins into a drawer, 'Guard, arrest this man.' One of the henchmen reached in through the door and clamped his enormous hand on Captain Ali's shoulder.

'What?' The Captain struggled to free himself, but although the giant was unable to get into the tiny space, he easily pinned his victim in place.

'What's the charge? I have done nothing wrong,'

'Releasing un-tethered animals to molest the town and disturbing the peace.' Simon Squiggle smiled.

'Ok,' said the Captain, 'what's the fine? ahaar'

'Oh, no fine,' the official's smile widened, 'the penalty is eventual death.'

'Eventual, what do you mean eventual death?'

'Oh it's like instant death but takes a little longer,' Squiggle smiled so wide his wart was squished into a fold in his face. 'I could of course overlook the matter I suppose.' His face returned to its usual dour expression. 'One hundred shillings.'

Captain Ali threw his purse onto the desk. The restraining hand released his shoulder and, grateful that he still had his shirt, the Captain turned to leave.

'Oh Captain,' Simon Squiggle's voice was sickly sweet, but it froze the Captain in his tracks. 'Was there something I could be of assistance with?'

Not daring to voice his thoughts Captain Ali muttered, 'Water, fresh water, for my ship.'

'No problem, my friend, leave it to me.'

Captain Ali Anxious re-joined the others who had witnessed the scene from outside but could not make out everything that was said. The Captain filled in the details as they walked into town.

'Don't worry Captain we will get even with him before we leave,' said Sally. The look on her face sent a chill down his spine but he had no doubt she would make good the threat and he felt better for that.

They went into the first restaurant they came across. Oil lamps burned in sconces on the walls and the sign at the entrance said: 'Harbour Inn. Cheese a Speciality.' The waiter was busy stacking chairs on top of the tables but looked up at the sound of the door creaking open.

'I was just closing for the night,' he said with a smile. 'The chef has already gone but you are welcome to a plate of bread and cheese if that will suffice?'

Half the town could hear Ben's tummy rumble as he seated himself at a table.

'Bring it on young man, ahaar.' He dribbled in anticipation. The others joined him pushing two tables together to make space for all.

'Bread and cheese all round it is then,' said Digby. 'What have you to drink?'

'I'm Julian and I will be your waiter for this evening,' said the waiter getting into his routine. 'Today's specials are cheese . . . er, just cheese. To drink we have sprout smoothies, rainwater cocktails or rust tea. What will be your pleasure this fine evening?'

'Sprout smoothies?' Norman said.

'One sprout smoothie, and for the ladies?'

'No, no, no,' Norman hastened to correct the waiter, 'no sprout smoothies. I'll try the rainwater cocktail. Girls?'

'Rust tea for me,' said Sally. The others chose the same except for the Captain.

'You wouldn't have a drop of cod liver oil by any chance, would you?' he asked without much conviction.

'Cod liver oil?' Julian threw up his hands in a theatrical gesture, 'Are you sure you can afford it, dear?'

'Er . . . is it very expensive?' the Captain only had a few coins that remained in his trouser pocket.

'Five shillings a shot, my bold Captain,' lisped the waiter.

'Five shillings! I have just given the harbourmaster a full bottle it must have been worth hundreds!'

'Oh, Slippery Simon Squiggle,' said the waiter. 'I wouldn't get on the wrong side of him.'

'I think I already am,' said the Captain. 'I think I'll just have the rust tea.'

'He is nasty bit of work then, this Slippery Simon,' said Digby.

'Oh if you only knew. He once got a Captain the death penalty because his animals escaped.'

'Er . . . what kind of animals?' the Captain asked.

'Only one actually, a sweet little pussycat.'

'Not apes then?' the Captain gulped.

'Oh were they yours?' Julian threw up his hands. 'They came right past here, scared the pants off me, I can tell you.'

'Sorry about that,' said the Captain. 'They are gentle creatures really.'

'Oh I know, but I am not used to such big things around my person. You needn't worry though; green apes are exempt from the regulations.' Julian minced off to get their order.

Once the waiter had finished bringing their meal Digby asked him to join them so that they could learn more of the ways of Ever-Rest. Julian made himself a Sprout smoothie and pulled up a chair between Digby and Prudence. Amid effuse admiration for Prue's dress designer and punctuation of his lisped sentences with little pats on Digby's knee, the young waiter filled them in on the main points for survival on the island.

It seemed that Everrestians usually slept from soon after the red sun had set to be fresh when the yellow day dawned, then they partied all night until the red sun came up again. It was way past Julian's bedtime by the time they were ready to go and Prudence helped him clear up the debris around Ben's place setting before they gave the waiter a substantial tip and bade him good night.

Shore Patrol.

They awoke to the sound of a horse and cart clattering to a halt on the cobblestoned quay. Digby peered out of the porthole.

'It is the water wagon,' he called to Prudence who, for once, had not got up before dawn.

'Oh, I haven't even cleaned the hold.' She jumped out of bed and pulled her dress on over her pyjamas.

'Don't worry,' said Digby, 'they are no doubt used to a bit of dust.'

By the time they arrived on deck, Knobby had the gangplank out and the first of the barrels was being rolled up it.

At the top Ben, still in his nightshirt, stopped the two emaciated looking labourers and made them stand the barrel up and open the lid. He dipped his hand in, scooped up some liquid and sipped.

'Phaa,' he spat it out again, 'sea water, ahaar. The little wretch has sent sea water, I'll have his . . .'

'Will you give your master my complements, ahaar,' the Captain spoke over the ex-pirate's tirade, 'and advise him that by some mistake your barrels contain sea water and we require fresh water.' Ben was still muttering bloodthirsty curses as the deliverymen returned the barrel to their cart and trundled off.

An hour later the water cart returned. Knobby checked each barrel before allowing it to be tipped into their tank. He declared the consignment to be sweet and clear. To the delight of the girls, normal washing regimes returned to shipboard life and by nightfall they were ready to go out on the town.

Leaving the Lexi dressed throughout with laundry

of all shapes and sizes festooning her rigging, they strode arm in arm into town. The difference from the previous night was dramatic. Happy citizens strolled along the boulevards gossiping, waving, and calling out to those they passed. Shop windows glowed with a myriad of oil lamps and candles illuminating a bewildering array of goods and produce.

'This is more like it,' said Sally, dragging Norman towards a display of dresses and underpinnings that drew her like a magnet. Ben, on the other end of their chain, was pulling towards the cheese emporium of the previous night. The link broke between Knobby and the Captain and, with a promise from the girls that they would not be long, it was agreed to meet for drinks at the Harbour Inn before moving on to explore the other eating establishments that now displayed their signs along the avenue.

With an enthusiasm, which bordered on reckless, Knobby joined the girls as they rifled through the wares offering opinions, making suggestions and even holding items up against his body so that they could see how they looked. Norm and Dig stood to one side a little embarrassed and pretending for the most part to be just idling in the street, only responding with a smile or a nod when one of the girls called them by name.

'Don't get me wrong,' said Digby in confidential tones, 'he is a great chap and all that, but Knobby worries me sometimes.'

'I know what you mean,' said Norman. 'I can't make him out either.'

Ben had already consumed a plate of cheese and the Captain was on his second glass of cod liver oil by the time the young people re-joined them. A round of rainwater cocktails was brought by Julian the waiter who, despite the fact that the restaurant was busy, insisted on seeing the girls' shopping. Knobby took on the task of showing him, much to the amusement of the other customers. The fashion show was cut short when the café owner, a rotund gentleman with a barnacled face, chivvied the animated Julian back to work.

'I think we should move on into town now,' said Norman. 'We can find somewhere for dinner later, what do you think Dig?'

'I agree, there is a lot to see here and we haven't gone a hundred metres past the harbour gate since we got here.' Digby looked around the table to gather a nodded response from all except for Ben who was fully occupied with a piece of cheddar as big as his fist.

Arm in arm once again they set off up the yellow brick road to wherever it led. Between the harbour gate and the inn, the shops and other establishments had been largely devoted to nautical things such as sail-makers, rope-makers, chandlers, and the like. There were occasional grog shops and more than a few bawdy houses in between.

'What is a bawdy house,' said Prudence, craning her neck to peer in the window of one such establishment.

'Ahem, er . . . it's a place where sea faring gentlemen go when they get bored,' the Captain replied, running his finger round his collar in a nervous fashion.

'Oh, perhaps we can go there when we get bored then,'

They let the matter drop, much to Digby's relief, and were soon adequately diverted by the delights of the market. Street entertainers abounded - jugglers, stilt walkers, clowns, fire-eaters and the like, all performing for a few coins. There was one thing conspicuous by its absence - music. Even a troupe of dancing girls, whose scanty costumes and golden nubile bodies intrigued all the male members of the group, gyrated and squirmed in an eerie silence.

Prudence made up her own tune and started to hum it as an accompaniment until a passing stranger whispered.

'I shouldn't let the secret police hear you singing. It is banned, don't you know?'

'Excuse me,' Digby caught the stranger by the sleeve, 'what do you mean banned?'

'Not allowed, singing is not allowed?'

'His Excellency the Governor put out a decree banning all music and singing in the street. It was supposedly because people were being kept awake at night, but we all know it was because he was beaten in a karaoke contest by a street singer.'

'Oh,' said Prudence, 'but I sing all the time. I can't help it.'

'Well, just keep an eye out for the secret police,' said the stranger.

'How do we do that if they are secret?' said Digby.

'Oh they are easy to spot, there is one now.' Without moving his eyes he gave an almost imperceptible nod. 'No! don't look now, anyone caught recognising them is arrested and never seen again.'

'Which one,' Digby whispered, trying hard not to look.

'All in black with a big raincoat and an armband,' the stranger replied out of the corner of his mouth.

'You mean the one with the ear trumpet and a giant floppy hat?' Prudence stared at the sinister figure as it went past.

'That's the one. They all dress like that. It is their uniform,' said the stranger.

'What is so secret about that?' said Digby in his normal voice once again.

'Ah,' said the stranger still from the corner of his mouth, 'that's a secret too.' He pulled away and disappeared into the crowd.

'I am beginning to dislike this place,' said Prudence. She picked up an apple off a nearby stall and polished it with the hem of her dress. 'I'll be glad when we can leave.'

'Me too,' said Digby, gently taking the shining fruit from her and returning it to the display. The stallholder offered them another but they moved away to follow their friends.

'Anyway,' said Digby, 'you could always get a job as an apple polisher if we have to stay too long.'

'Don't even suggest it,' said Prudence. 'Come on, let's eat. The others have stopped at that vegetarian restaurant over there.'

Fine Dining.

The group gathered around the bill of fare displayed on a stand outside the entrance to the restaurant.

'Did you say this is a vegetarian restaurant?' Prudence asked as she studied the list. 'These seem to be all meat dishes to me.'

'Cow burger, Ostrich burger, Camel burger, Yak burger,' recited Digby. 'This is just an Ever-Rest version of Mackdoodles. They even have Eggy-Mackmufti on the menu.'

'Yes and Limburger,' said Ben. 'I love Limburger Cheese.'

'Oh no, not Limburger,' said Prudence 'it smells like Digby's socks.'

'I thought you loved my feet,' said Digby.

'Ssh,' said Prudence blushing, then in a whisper, 'feet yes, socks no.'

'Never the less that is what I will have,' said Ben.

'It seems strange that the next option is Limburger with cheese,' said Norman stroking his wart.

'Oh come on, let's go in, I'm starving,' said Sally and led the way.

Inside there were tables and chairs to either side of a central aisle which led to a row of counters at the back, each manned by a bored looking young person in a less than flattering uniform and wearing a small cap.

'It's a self-service, just like Mackydoo's at home,' said Sally and she headed for a counter where the assistant displayed a line of five yellow stars on her chest.

'Hello, I'm Muriel, what can I get you today?' said the longest serving assistant. (She had been three times assistant of the month in the last five years.)

'Yes, but first can you tell me why this is advertised as a vegetarian restaurant when nearly all the menu is meat?' Sally thought she would get the matter cleared up right from the start.

'I dunno,' said Muriel, 'shall I call the manager?' and before Sally could tell her not to bother, screeched out, 'Mr Grimsdale!'

A slightly older youth covered in acne spots, some of which were bigger than his wart, ambled over. To be fair about his skin condition, the spots were quite diminutive, but then so was his wart.

'What's the matter Muriel?' said Mr Grimsdale without a glance at the group of customers gathered at the counter.

'This lady,' Muriel said the word like an insult, 'wants to know why it says this is a vegetarian restaurant.'

'Oh, a troublemaker eh,' said the manager, looking for the first time at Sally.

'No, no,' said Sally, 'just curious. It doesn't matter really, we like meat anyway.'

'It's part of our healthy eating campaign,' said Grimsdale, melting before the good looks and assertive manner of the young woman who confronted him. 'W, we g... g... guarantee that all the meat we serve is stripped from the discarded carcases of nothing but pure vegetarian animals, a... a... and we put a bit of wilted lettuce in each bun.'

'Oh I see,' said Sally, 'in that case I'll have an Eggy Mackmufti and chips.'

'Eggy-Mack and fries,' said the manager, 'write that down before you forget it Muriel.' He was then called away to deal with a small fire in the kitchen.

Muriel took their remaining orders, greeting each new request with the response, 'do you want to go large with that?' In the background a measure of chaos could be detected as various members of the kitchen staff appeared momentarily around the corner, some blackened with soot, others singed and smoking and, in one case, with a wisp of flame coming from his hair. Muriel ignored this completely and, with one carefully formed letter at a time, wrote their order on the board in front of her. She then went back and forth to the rack behind her to search among the pre-packed items for a box of the right colour. She ticked off the ones she found and screeched at the kitchen staff for ones she did not. She scooped splinters of fried potatoes into envelopes and propped them up on the tray between the cartons of chilled drinks so that they would be cold by the time it came to eat them, then stood picking the dirt out from behind her fingernails with a fork while she waited for the last two orders to arrive.

'Eggy-Mack,' came a cry from the smoke laden kitchen, closely followed by 'Limbo,' in a different voice from the same place. Muriel threw the fork back in the tray alongside her till position and ambled back to pick up the boxes. Prudence could not resist retrieving the offending piece of cutlery and giving it a damn good polish.

After an interminable delay while Muriel calculated their bill and dismissed them with a droned 'enjoy your meal,' the boys carried the laden trays to a vacant table. Prudence went ahead and removed the debris left by the previous occupants and scrubbed the surface with a cloth purloined from one of the cleaners who, despite the fact that he was using it on another table, didn't notice it was gone until she returned it.

From the heap of cardboard and paper containers that they stacked neatly into a tower on the middle of the table, they passed them out and opened them one by one to examine their food.

'Mine is wrong,' said Ben. 'It says Limburger on the box but it is just a meat patty, ahaar.'

'It has got cheese on it' said Knobby as he lifted his Yak Burger with both hands, struggling to contain the yoghurt that oozed out of all sides of the bun. Ben lifted the top off his and sniffed, 'that's not even Limburger cheese either,' he said.

'Thank goodness,' muttered Prudence.

'Ahoy there, matey,' Ben caught the arm of the manager as he was hurrying past with a fire bucket in each hand, 'This is supposed to be Limburger. All I've got is mousetrap.' He waved the bun under Mr Grimsdale's nose.

'That is correct Sir,' the spotty youth replied. 'A burger made entirely of limbs, what did you expect, Limburger Cheese? ha ha, that would cost an arm and a leg around here.

'Oh,' said Ben, 'er . . . what kind of limbs?' The manager just shrugged and remembering the urgency of his mission rushed off to the scene of the fire, splashing water on the way. The cleaner, apparently working on his own initiative, put down his mop and bucket and went off to a cupboard and brought out an A-frame notice board stating *Danger Wet Floor* and placed it near the spillage and went back to cleaning tables.

Sally's Eggy came with a small paper poncho that she donned before opening her package. Inside she found a steaming ostrich egg with a yoke the size of a teacup. She took up one of her fries and plunged it into the yolk. The resultant eruption splattered the front of her bib in sticky yellow goo, which also spread in a semicircle of speckles that covered half the table. Unabashed, she placed the coated chip in her mouth.

'Boy, that is to die for,' she declared, licking her lips.

'You probably would if you made that mess on Prue's table on the Lexi, ahaar,' said Ben, spraying bun crumbs to join the yolk in front of them.

'The cagoule is a good idea though,' said Prudence. 'Perhaps we can get one for you, Ben.' They fell silent as they tucked into their boxes of delight and at the end they agreed  that, despite its dubious origins, the food was delicious.

They left the restaurant just as the fire department arrived and glanced back to realise that the faint sign above the door now revealed, in the flickering flame that was about to engulf it, the words: *Muckydidles, for flame grilled burgers.* At least that didn't transgress the trade description act any more.

In the Inn.

It had been a week now since their arrival in Ever-Rest and, as another cheery golden day under the northern sun followed a depressing day and night of the red southern version, Digby was anxious to move on.

'Why can't we just slip our moorings and creep out at night,' he asked the Captain.

'Have ye seen the size o' them cannons on the fjord walls? They'll blow us out of the water.'

'But we can't wait here forever,' Digby complained.

'I've heard tales o' those who tried that would make your wart turn inside out, ahaar,' replied the Captain.

'Surely, they are exaggerated,' challenged Digby.

'Maybe they are, maybe not. Perhaps ye'd better come along with me to the Sticky Seaman and hear first-hand, ahaar.'

'Perhaps we all had,' said Digby.

'Look ye, the rough bars of the waterfront are no place for delicate young ladies,' said Captain Anxious, 'but call Norm if ye've a mind tae, aye, the sun will be over the yardarm in an hour and the boys would be gatherin', ahaar. Knobby are you coming?'

'Right with ye Cap'n,' said the mate.

Digby thought of challenging that inference, as he knew Prue and Sally would. He defied any man to stand up to them if they were riled, but he had to agree that he would rather do this without them.

The 'Sticky Seaman' used to be called the 'Anchor and Barnacle' until shortly after Ben and the Captain started frequenting it. A hastily painted sign had been hung over the original in honour of the tale the crew of the Lexi told with such gusto.

It consisted of a large bar room full of crude wooden tables and bench seats, the wall to one side lined with barrels and the opposing one fitted as a bar with a castellated counter top to defend the supply of Cod-liver Oil stored behind it.

'Ho-ho, welcome Captain Cake-hole,' came the ribald cheer as the four of them entered. Ben was already established with a pint of Grog and a plate of cheese. Captain Ali doffed his tricorn hat to the assembled seafarers and they joined Ben at his table.

'You found your supply of Limburger, I gather.' Digby sniffed the air as he sat opposite the old sea dog.

'I regret not, young Sir, ahaar, that be me socks, aye, ahaar.' Ben sprayed cheese with relaxed impunity in the absence of Prudence. Digby slid down the bench to be out of range of at least one of the onslaughts.

The bar was quite busy with seafaring types partaking of a liquid breakfast or the hair of the dog. Most were pretty scurvy looking and the predominance of vicious looking knives sticking out of their belts made the young men nervous. A buxom wench wearing a short skirt and low-necked blouse took their order. The options being grog, cheese, bread, and for those that could afford it cod liver oil. All conversation around them stopped when Norman asked for a rainwater cocktail.

'Ahaar,' laughed Captain Ali, 'just a joke my dear, it'll be grogs all round, aye lads? ahaar.' The girl went over to the barrels and started to pour four rusty tankards of brown liquid.

'Are ye trying to ruin my reputation,' the Captain hissed.

'But it is only the second hour of the day,' Norman protested.

'Just drink your grog and look tough,' said the Captain.

The waitress delivered their drinks, banging them down on the table causing the contents to spill onto the surface around them. The muddy liquid, on contact with the wood, began to froth and bubble until it evaporated leaving a scorch mark to join the many others that overlaid its surface.

'Gowan me hearties, get 'em down yer,' the waitress said with a wink that, without a doubt, was directed at Digby.

'This is one of the few places where the serving wenches don't say "enjoy your meal or have a nice day," ahaar,' said Ben, 'that's why we love it, aye.' He sent the waitress on her way with a little pat on her ample bottom.

'D'ye sees that man that just came in? ahaar' said the Captain, 'that be Lloyd Lloyd, the sea brigand. He used to be the terror of all commercial seafarers until he went into banking. He owns the Black Horse. She be riding at anchor in the middle of the harbour when we arrived, ahaar.'

'Ahoy there, shipmate.' With a cursory flick of his hand, the newcomer dismissed the waitress that rushed to attend him and strode through the room towards them. He was tall and ramrod straight with a pointy face below his feathered tricorn hat. A thin black moustache adorned his upper lip with a wart the size of a peach to the left side. On reaching them, he removed a large gleaming white handkerchief from the frilly sleeve of his smart green jacket and dusted the cheese crumbs off the bench and settled his white breeches down on the bench next to Digby.

'Limburger?' he enquired.

'Old socks,' said Digby in reply.

'Hmm,' said he, 'you must be the Sticky Bun Kid I've heard so much about. Permit me to introduce myself. I am Captain Lloyd, the Sea Banker.' He handed Digby a card emblazoned with the emblem of a black horse and the legend Lloyd TSB. 'Perhaps you have a treasure you wish to deposit?'

'Well, n, no, not at the moment.' Digby replied

'Never mind, I'm sure you will have soon judging from what I've heard. Keep the card. You can always use our on-line banking service when you are at sea.'

'On line banking?' Digby enquired.

'Yes we meet you at sea and you trail your treasure in a net on the end of a long line and we come up and collect it from there. It saves the risk of being boarded don't ye know.'

'Captain Lloyd, could you spare a moment? ahaar,' said Captain Anxious. Kindly explain to these young gentlemen the perils of leaving this here port without permission?'

'I wouldn't even countenance it,' Lloyd replied. 'I have the most powerful ship ever to grace the ocean and I would never risk it. Even if they didn't sink you, those guns will tear your sails to shreds and you would be washed away over the waterfall at the end of the world before you could bend on new ones. Am I right Ali?'

'That ye are, Cap'n Lloyd, that ye are.'

Now, if you will excuse me Gentlemen, I have an IMF meeting in the back room and I see the delegates are gathering.' He stood and, nodding to a group of men that had entered the inn, 'It was good meeting you, young Digby and you Norman the Knocker, I presume. Perhaps we can do business some time.' He stalked off to disappear with the others through a door at the far end of the bar.

'Now d'ye see,' said Captain Anxious, 'this inn is frequented by the roughest, toughest bunch of sea going rogues you can find, cut throats, murderers, thieves, pirates, bankers and aye, even insurance salesmen, and I tell ye none of them would risk them guns out there, ahaar.'

'I suppose you're right,' said Digby. 'But I . . .'

The door burst open

with a crash and in walked a dozen large men all armed with cutlasses, knives and clubs.

'Hogwash!' exclaimed the Captain.

'Oh, it's not so bad when you get used to it,' said Norman as he drained his mug of grog.

'Captain Hogwash,' Digby would have known it even without the Captain's reference as several of the new comers still had Prue's pink and blue icing clinging to their hair and beards.

'Hide,' said Ben as he slid under the table. Norman, Knobby and Digby joined him to find the Captain already there.

'D 'you think he saw us?' whispered Norman.

'Dunno,' hissed Digby, already feeling faint due to his proximity to Ben's socks.

Bankers Rest.

The ribald laughter that greeted Captain Horatio Hogwash as he entered the inn did not improve his mood any more than had the improvised sign above the door. After all, he was surrounded by sticky seamen and the cry of 'Hello Horace, we thought you were too stuck up to visit us, was just the icing on the cake. He swore that if ever he set eye, for he only had the one, on that lily-livered Captain of the Lexi, he would run him through and his crew with him, a task he fully intended to stick to. He glared at the assembled sea dogs that jeered and joked at his expense. A single barrelled glare, nevertheless silenced the majority of them. Seeing the one vacant table, Hogwash pushed his way towards it. With one hand on his cutlass and the other shoving or slapping the heads of the cutthroats on the benches in-between, he came ever closer to where the Lexi crew were hiding.

'Grog,' he yelled across the room at the waitress by the barrels then, at the sight of the cheese peppered table, he added, 'and fetch a cloth; this table is disgusting.'

'Look who's talking, ahaar,' said a muffled voice.

'Aye, Horatio can't sit at a sticky table, now can he lads?' an anonymous jibe from behind. He spun around but missed the culprit amongst the grinning faces.

'He should be used to it by now,' came another heckle from the opposite direction. Like an enraged bull he kicked the bench back, sat and swung his legs in, clipping Ben in the ear with his toe.

'Ouch!' yelled Ben.

'What the . . .' Horatio peered into the gloom 'Ben Bun, I should have guessed by the mess. Phew is that Limburger?' he had come into range of the old hand's feet.

Ben, for his part, was squirming to the far side of the table but, on realising he was discovered, leapt to his feet shouting, 'Surprise!'

The table tipped forward spilling its contents of grog, cheese crumbs and all into the hapless Horatio's lap. This also revealed the other Urlanders skulking there.

'Run!' yelled Norman and they were off like a small herd of gazelle, leaping over benches and jumping from table to table as they made for the door.

Hogwash followed like a rhino in heat, barging his way through the tables and chaotic crowd.

'Fleet-footed Norman was in the lead, head down and at full tilt until he bounced off of something soft and springy. It was the first mate of the Black Pig. A mountain of a man, he blocked the doorway, not out of quick witted anticipation but, instead, by virtue of being too slow to get out of the way. Norman's head-butt into his rotund belly had little or no effect, neither did the secondary impact of the rest of the crew who were too close to pull up and clattered into the human drawbridge.

'Avast there, grab them,' bellowed the charging rhino. Huge but ponderous arms swept down threatening to engulf the frantic four but they had time to recover and duck out of the way. Not so for the pursuer. Cutlass in hand and with a bigger head of steam than a locomotive, Hogwash crashed headlong into his henchman. The point of his weapon buried itself deep into the solid oak of the inn door and only a millimetre below the big man's crotch. At the sight of this, the giant fainted clean away, collapsing on top of his Captain and pinning him to the floor.

In ongoing panic, the little group of startled springboks bounced round the room until, now following Captain Ali's lead, they burst through the small door to the private room at the back.

The meeting of the IMF was in full swing. Captain Lloyd and various other distinguished members of the Ingenuous Moneymaking Fun club were seated around a large round table in the centre of the luxuriously appointed room. Loud music was playing and the bankers were all chanting and passing round a plate with a huge chocolate gateau on it. The sudden appearance of the fugitives brought the festivities to a sudden halt.

Silence hung in the air like smoke on a still day until it was cleared by Captain Lloyd. 'Captain Anxious!' he exclaimed, 'what a surprise. Permit me to introduce you to the boys.' He pushed the cake into the centre of the table and called to the waitress. 'Bring some more chairs for our guests and drinks all round,' Then in a lower voice, 'Put them on the Captain's bill.'

Captain Anxious was relieved to hear Ben slam home the bolts on the door. Encumbered somewhat by Norman and Digby jostling at his elbow, Ali doffed his hat in a low bow.

'Sorry to intrude on your . . . ahem, conference gentlemen, but we are being pursued by a substantial band of bloodthirsty brigands and this is our only escape route, ahaar.'

'Not at all my dear fellow, come in and rest awhile, you look quite flushed,' A portly gentleman on the opposite side of the table stood to return the bow. 'My name is Nathaniel, banker for the western isles.' He bowed low, twirling his fork with a flourish, 'May I present my esteemed associate Harry of Spend Borrow and Cheat.' He indicated his colleague sitting to his left who was wearing a large bib and a napkin tucked into the belt of his plus-fours. 'If you will excuse me gentlemen I must deal with a small matter outside.' He strode past them towards the door from which loud hammering and shouting could be heard.

'Be careful, Sir, they are heavily armed,' warned Norman.

'And sticky,' Digby added with a smirk.

'Well at least I'm dressed for it' said Harry with a wink. Despite his generous proportions, Harry moved with feline grace. Not just because all his contracts had hidden in the fine print a short statement on how much he expected to be paid, but because of his whole confident demeanour. His lazy stroll and purring voice could not disguise the presence of claws ready to spring from his velvet touch. No doubt he had a similar clause in all his dealings. HSBC as he was affectionately known, threw back the bolts, flung open the door and stood in the portal.

'What is the meaning of this?' he roared. The pussycat had become a lion; standing legs astride and fists akimbo he cut a dramatic figure, his bib swung round behind him like a cape.

Hogwash staggered back in surprise but recovered quickly.

'Let me at them muck slinging lily-livered swabs,' demanded the irate pirate.

'Desist!' countered the banker. 'What kind of behaviour is this for a seagoing gentleman. You ought to be ashamed of yourself.'

Somewhat abashed, Captain Horatio tried to protest but the caped banker would have none of it. Eventually the brigand slunk away, muttering threats under his breath and cursing at the crowd of jeering onlookers who found the whole incident most amusing.

Kidnapped.

When HSBC re-joined the party, Nathaniel of the West and Lloyd TSB had completed the introductions. 'I was just saying,' said Captain Ali, 'that it is very good of you to come to our rescue like this . . . er . . . ahaar.'

'Not at all old chap, we of the financial community recognise one of our own when we see one,' replied Harry. 'Accountant isn't it? By the way, you can drop the yo- ho- ho- isms here.'

'Thank goodness for that,' said Ali, 'I do have trouble remembering.'

The four Urlanders took to the extra chairs at the table and the drinks were passed round.

'I'm sorry, we seemed to have interrupted the cake cutting,' said Digby. 'Somebody's birthday is it?'

'No, not at all. It is a game we play,' Lloyd replied. 'We were just starting. Perhaps you would like to join in. It is called "Have your Cake and Eat It"'

Digby looked at the huge thick disk of patisserie and licked his lips. 'I'm in,' he said.

'How do we play?,' said Norman suspiciously.

'It's quite simple,' Busby Barclay chimed in. 'One person provides a cake.' He pushed the cake over in front of Norman. 'When the music starts we pass the cake around the table. 'The musician is blindfolded so he can't see where the plate is.'

'That accounts for the rubbish music,' whispered Ben.

'When the music stops,' Busby continued, 'the banker has to cut as big a piece of cake as he can eat in thirty seconds. When the music starts, the cake is moved on. If he hasn't eaten all his slice of the cake he is said to have failed and drops out of the game with a nice sticky bun as a bonus. This is repeated until there is no cake left or, by chance, it lands in the lap of the original cake provider in which case he can keep what is left. If all the cake is eaten, then the provider is out on his ear . . . Do you want to play?

'Well . . .' Norman stroked his wart.

'Oh, come on Norm,' Digby pleaded. 'That cake looks delicious.'

'All right, just one round.'

'Good, said Busby. 'Waitress, put that cake on his bill.' The music started and the cake was whisked away.

Three cakes later the bankers were all stuffed to the gills. Their faces were covered in icing and cream.

Ali called a halt to the proceedings saying there were duties and they must get back to ship.

'So soon, said Harry. 'We have another game that might fix your interest.'

'I'm not sure we can afford any more fun,' said Ali as he paid the bill. 'But thank you once again for coming to our aid.'

'Yes,' said Norman. 'We are indeed in your debt.'

'You are welcome to be in our debt any time,' said Harry.

'We don't know how we could ever thank you,' said Digby.

'Well . . . perhaps in return you might impart the secret of your remarkable ammunition,' suggested

Lloyd. 'We could make it worth your while.' He stroked his wart as he spoke.

'Obviously I would have to discuss this with my shareholders, but we could maybe come to an accommodation.' Ally replied. Perhaps a franchise or licensing agreement could be arranged. What do you think Digby?' He looked at his friend who was staring off into the distance.

'What? Well yes, I suppose, but it would be up to Prue with regard to the icing; only she knows how it is made. And it is Ben's recipe for the cakes.'

'Where is Ben by the way?' asked Captain Ali. Digby just nodded in the direction he was staring. Captain Ali followed his eyes to discover Ben stalking after a waitress who was carrying a redundant cheesecake back to the kitchen.

'There is just one thing I should warn you about,' said Harry, a serious look for once on his chocolate-rimmed face. 'Hogwash is not about to give up on his vendetta and, if this young lady holds the secret of the stickiness, I would have her guarded day and night if I were you.'

'Prue!' Digby exclaimed. 'We left her and Sally alone on the Lexi, we'd better get back.' He leapt up and, dragging Ali by the wrist, fought his way through the revellers to the door collecting Norm, Knobby and Ben on the way. After another stampede across the newly re-laid tables, they burst into the street. With the cry of 'You're barred,' from the disgruntled landlord unheeded, Digby led them onto the quayside.

'What is it?' panted Norman as they skittered to a stop alongside their vessel. Digby looked up at the deck. All seemed quiet.

'Nothing I hope,' he replied. Cupping his hands around his mouth, he yelled, 'Prue . . . Sally.' A chill ran up his spine when, after a full minute, no response came from the girls. Followed by the now anxious Norman he ran up the gangplank. The chill that had previously run up Digby's spine made the return journey almost precipitating an undesirable reaction in his bowels. A red stain on the deck near the gangplank led to a trail of similar hue across the deck to where a scramble net was still hanging over the side. Out in the harbour, the ominous shape of the Black Pig lay at anchor alongside the Black Horse, looking like a watery farmyard in the middle of the harbour. Carried on the still afternoon air, the sound of lurid sea shanties drifted across the two hundred metres of open water. A sudden scream pierced the air before being cut off abruptly. Digby supported his pale friend at the rail with a steadying arm, even though he was feeling weak at the knees himself.

'Don't worry mate, we'll get them back,' he said, fingering his left wart with his free hand.

'How?' Norman gripped the rail, his knuckles gleaming white. 'There are dozens of them over there; I can see them from here.'

'We'll get help lad,' Captain Anxious had arrived. Breathless as he was, he had appraised the situation with a glance. 'We'll get help.'

Knobby was assisting the apoplectic Ben up the gangplank; the dash from the inn had almost done for the old mariner.

'We need a plan,' said Digby, fingering his other wart this time.

'They'd better not hurt them!' Norman spoke through clenched teeth.

'More bad news,' said Knobby from the after deck. 'Our dinghy is missing.'

Demands with Menaces

Captain Ali dashed into his cabin. 'Knobby,' he roared, 'take this note to Captain Lloyd at the Sticky Seaman. He quickly, for an accountant very quickly, wrote a message on a torn-out page from the log and handed it to the mate. Knobby looked at it, but it was encoded in financial double talk with so many 'party of the first parts' and 'to whit hence forths' that he could not understand it.

'Move yourself,' shouted the Captain in a most uncharacteristic fit of assertiveness. Knobby was galvanised into action, charging down the gangplank at a reckless pace and knocking the pirate coming the other way straight on his backside. Not stopping to help the unfortunate brigand up, Knobby yelled, 'stand by to repel boarders,' and continued his headlong dash to find the sea banker.

The remaining crew ran to the top of the gangplank, weapons in hand. The pirate got to his feet, rubbed his posterior, and spoke.

'I have a message from my Captain.' He brandished a scrap of paper threateningly.

'Hogwash?' said Captain Ali.

'No. I really do,' said the pirate.

'Is it from Captain Hogwash?' said Norman.

'Oh aye, ahaar, that it be.' The pirate had regained his composure and his pirate's inflection.

'Come aboard, and no funny business,' roared the Captain.

'What funny business?' said Norman.

'Well I thought Knobby knocking him on his bum quite funny,' chuckled Ben.

They took the note from the sultry seaman and, while Digby and Captain Anxious read it, Norman and Ben crowded close to the messenger in case he should make a run for it.

Er . . . is there any reply, er . . . ahaar.' The pirate had to gulp before he spoke. Digby's face had turned red. He drew his cutlass.

'If they do anything to harm my Prudence I'll - I'll . . .' he advanced on the pirate.

'If you hurt me it might compromise the integrity of the contract . . . ahaar.'

'You weren't always a pirate were you,' said Norman restraining the young man with one hand and fending off his friend with the other.

N... no... I was a solicitor's clerk actually, but I joined up for a life of adventure. Now I'm stuck. They won't let me go back er . . . ahaar?

'What's your name?' snapped Digby, the tip of his blade inches from the pirate's throat.

'P... P... P... Peter Penworthy,' he replied, his Adams apple bobbing about like a mouse in a sock.

'Well, listen to me, Penworthy,' said Digby. 'You tell Captain Hogwash that we are coming to get our girls back and if any harm should befall them he will only live long enough to wish he was dead.' He paused to ponder his own words, not sure if they came out right. Satisfied, he bopped the young pirate in the nose with the flat side of his sword. 'Now get ye gone . . . ahaar, indeed.'

Captain Ali had written a hasty message which he handed to the messenger.

'Ok boys, let him go,' he said. 'Peter, that note is for Prudence's eyes only, right, and if you get a chance to help our ladies it might help to get you back to that nice peaceful solicitors office, ahaar?'

A thoughtful ex-clerk stepped slowly down the gangplank and then ran off down the harbour as if being chased by a dog. Until, that is, he clattered into Knobby coming with equal velocity the other way.

Knobby joined them in the cabin, still laughing at the fate of Captain Hogwash's messenger. The impact which, incidentally, put Knobby on his backside, tipped Penworthy over the quayside wall. He was last seen swimming towards the pirate ship in the middle of the harbour.

'Now, down to business.' Captain Ali Anxious exerted his newfound authority. 'This is serious.' They studied the note spread out on the table in front of them.

> *Yower gyrl will nay be armed if ye bring the recipee for the ard baked aminition to the middle of the arbour at midnyght. Also cend a note telling er that she must* ~~dyvlulge~~ *tell the cecret of her eyecing.*
> *Sined*

Captyng Horatio Hogwash PHD

'I see Horatio has invested in a spell checker since last we had written communications,' said Captain Ali.

'What's PHD stand for?' asked Norman.

'Pretty Hard Dude' said Ben. 'He always puts that; he thinks it gives him a degree of authority.'

'What did you put in the note,' said Digby, 'Did you tell Prue to give him the recipe,'

'Yes, in a way I did,' the captain replied, 'but I told her not to divulge the secret ingredient, gunpowder.'

'But Hogwash is bound to read the note first and put it in himself,' said Knobby. Captain Ali nodded sagely.

'Hang on,' said Norman. 'There isn't any gunpowder in Prue's recipe.'

'Nor in my rock cakes,' added Ben. Ali Anxious just sat back and smiled.

Treachery

Knobby rowed the borrowed dinghy out into the dark area between the harbour and the pirate ship. Captain Ali Anxious sat straight and stern in the stern. In the back of the small boat coming the other way in the gloom, he could make out three shadowy figures.

'Ahoy Anxious,' the voice was that of horrible Horatio Hogwash PHD

'Avast there Hogwash,' Captain Ali replied, 'Let me see the ladies before you heave to, ahaar.' There was a brief delay as the oarsmen in the pirate's dinghy shipped oars and dragged two dark shapes upright from the middle of the boat. A sack had been tied over their heads. They struggled against the grip of the burly pirates, oblivious of the risk of falling overboard.

'Are you all right me dears,' Ali called. A muffled unintelligible voice carried to him. It had a definite female timbre to it.

'We had to gag them, ahaar,' called Hogwash. 'They never stop nagging otherwise. Come alongside and you can have them aye and good riddance.' Knobby closed the distance with a few deft strokes then shipped his oars. The two vessels slid side by side, their gunwales grated against each other. Hands grabbed the rails and locked them together.

'Hand over the recipe,' Hogwash growled.

'The girls first,' Ali replied, his voice equally gruff.

'You can have this one first, and then I get the paper, right.' Hogwash poked at the bagged-up girl with his cutlass causing her to tumble towards the other boat.

'Agreed.' Ali caught the struggling figure and murmured, 'it's alright, it's me'

He held the rolled-up recipe in one hand and Hogwash snatched it from him. Ali cradled the girl as she tumbled headfirst into the bottom of his boat. The pirate that had been holding the craft together pushed them apart causing the dinghy to rock almost to the point of capsizing. By the time they had regained their equilibrium, the other crew were pulling strongly towards their mother ship.

'What about the other girl ye lubber,' Captain Ali yelled. He knew it was hopeless to pursue.

'Ye can have her back when she has whipped up a batch of ammunition to prove this works ahaar.'

Knobby was busy untying Sally. 'It seems our little plan has backfired,' he said ruefully.

'Aye, and so will their oven when that recipe goes in and our Prudence will blow with it, ahaar.'

'I hope you have a plan B,' said Sally as the gag was removed from her mouth.

'Er . . . no,' said Captain Ali, nodding his head vigorously.

'What, no plan B?' Sally exclaimed. 'You always have to have a plan B.'

'This was plan B,' said Knobby. 'Next we have plan . . .'

'Sssssh . . .' hissed the Captain. Then in a loud voice, 'Ok Knobby, let's go home.' He turned to look at the young woman, 'Did they hurt you?' he asked.

'No, not really. They were a bit rough but we gave as good as we got.'

'How about Prudence? We found blood on the deck of the Lexi.'

'Oh, that was Prue. She stuck one on the nose of their first mate. A better right cross I have never seen. He still had a set of keys down his back and a wad of cotton wool up his hooter when we left.'

Knobby struck out with the oars and they were soon alongside the Lexi again.

'Quick Sally, up the ladder, across the deck and down the other side. Knobby, you go and put a light in the cabin window then catch us up.' Captain Ali led the way. He knew that his adversary would be watching their movements through his powerful telescope. They would be silhouetted clearly against the lights of the harbour so, once on deck, he bent his knees and crouched progressively lower to pretend that he was going down stairs. Sally and Knobby followed suit.

'No need for you to pretend,' the Captain said to his mate. 'You really are going below. But keep your head down when you come back up, ahaar.'

'Aye aye Cap'n,' Knobby chuckled as he descended the companionway to the cabins.

Captain Ali Anxious and Sally Swift kept low until the bulk of the ship hid them from view then, holding Sally by the hand, he led her along the quayside.

'What exactly is plan B,' she asked as he paused at the end of their vessel to peer across the water at the enemy ship. Oh, you'll see he replied. Ok, get ready. Now run! The pair dashed across the brightly lit intervening space between their ship and the next then kept right on down the quay towards the Sticky Seaman.

To the Rescue

Knobby caught them up as they reached the doors of the pub. From within the inn the noise was intense. Despite the ban on music, sea shanties were being sung but, as the singers were all tone deaf and their voices out of tune, any semblance to music was purely lip service. Captain Anxious felt a certain amount of trepidation as he reached for the door handle, then he felt pain as the door burst open, bonking him on the nose and bowling him backwards onto his bottom in a most undignified manner. The League of Bankers he had called upon to help him appeared to be drunk as parrots on port and lemon and groggy as guillemots on grog. They tumbled through the entrance, staggered into the street and rolled into the road. With them they also rolled four large barrels.

Sally and Knobby helped their Captain to his feet. The tall figure of the Captain of the Black Horse swayed towards them. His seaman's gait had given way to a bank roll which threatened to capsize him.

'Ssssssh,' he hissed holding a finger to his lips and bending forward from his ankles to place his face within inches of Ali's. 'I'm as sober as an undertaker's underpants.' His clothes were spattered with cod liver oil and, as he tilted his head, grog trickled from the corner of his tricorn hat.

'What's going on Lloyd,' Ali asked.

'It's a party!' Captain Lloyd said, waving his arms about and then collapsing into those of his fellow officer. 'Hogwash has spies on the quayside. Quick, go inside and get changed or you'll miss the boat.' He allowed Ali to push him upright and, with an exaggerated bow to Sally that almost tipped him over, he staggered off to follow his receding crew. 'I must supervise the loading of our little carry out,' he yelled over his shoulder as he went. On the quayside, the crew were loading the barrels, with all the exaggerated care and clumsiness that is a by-product of intoxication, onto a fleet of longboats tied up against the harbour wall.

Captain Ali led the way inside. Shortly they reappeared significantly transformed. They merged in amongst a further contingent of renegade revellers. Captain Ali Anxious had shed his dress uniform coat and ruffled shirt with its ink stained cuffs in favour of a Sloppy Joe jumper slopped with slops from the slop bucket behind the bar. On his head was a banana coloured bandanna and, with a patch over his eye, he was changed from a sophisticated Captain cum three parts accountant of the seagoing variety into a three sheets to the wind sea dog of the inebriated variety. Sally had changed into a barmaid's costume augmented for her piece of mind with a cutlass concealed in her bustle and a shiv in her stocking. Knobby had no need to change his seaman's attire. He simply tipped a tankard of grog over his head and another down his throat, purely for authenticity he explained.

The trio joined one of the waiting longboats which immediately cast off. The crews rowed, some expertly, some not, causing a suitable level of chaos and confusion. A chorus of 'Roll Out the Barrel' bellowed out by the bilious bullies was at risk of becoming tuneful, but it was punctuated with curses, laughter and shouted orders enough to escape the attentions of the music police.

The flotilla followed a fickle course flitting fitfully from one side to the other of the direction they intended to follow. Some zigged whilst others zagged but their zigzag course led inexorably to the mooring that was shared by Captain Lloyd's ship, The Black Horse and The Black Pig of Captain Hogwash.

The crew of the Black Pig had already lost their gruntle and soon lost their tempers as the noisy returning revellers disturbed their disgruntled rest. They commenced to shout abuse calling the fun farers bankers and similar sounding insults.

'Now don't be like that, me hearties,' Captain Lloyd called back. 'Lower a rope and we'll send you up a barrel or two and you can join us in our celebration.'

'What ye celebratin' ahaar?'

'Oh, it's a fiscal holiday.'

'What's a fiscal?'

'Mostly they call "bloop, bloop, bloop."'

The mood changed, ropes were lowered and in the event four barrels were hoisted onto The Black Pig and a party was soon in full swing. Everyone was drinking and carousing, telling corny jokes and salty tales and having a high old time in the manner of low life scum the world over. Everybody, that is except Peter Penworthy the penitent pirate who was not in a party mood. It did not go beyond his notice that, over on the Black Horse, the crew seemed to spill nearly all their grog and soon settled down to sleep. The pirates on the other hand, including their esteemed but still horrible Captain, hogged as much grog as they could gulp.

It wasn't until close to dawn that the pirates, whose capacity for grog was extremely capacious, began to collapse. One by one, they discovered it difficult to keep drinking or even stand up and settled down in various positions on deck to sleep it off.

At last, all was quiet except for a slight grating noise which seemed to be coming from one of the barrels. Peter, still alert and sober, watched in silence. The end of the barrel slowly unscrewed and then, with a loud clatter, fell off.

Over on the Black Horse, hidden in the wheelhouse, Sally and Captain Lloyd watched and winced as the sound of barrel on deck rang out. Several of the somnolent seamen on the pirate ship stirred but settled again. Apparently sleeping on the deck of the banker's vessel was Captain Ali. He had cut a small hole in his eye-patch through which he could observe the nearby craft with his other eye closed.

A shadowy figure emerged from the open-ended barrel. The ends of the other two were turning now and he crept over to assist the nearest one. Captain Ali caught his breath as another shape emerged from the shadows and ran to the third barrel. Ali surreptitiously prepared for action but the unknown figure eased the lid to the deck and assisted the occupant out. Four figures now stood on the deck of the Black Pig. Norman, Digby and Ben stretched their limbs, cramped and stiff from their confinement in the false bottoms of the grog barrels.

A clever carpenter called Charlie and a crafty cooper called Colin had conceived the cunning contrivance and combined their considerable craftsmanship to construct the concealed contraptions.

Silently, Norman clasped Peter's hand and pointed to the hatch that led to the galley. Peter nodded his agreement. They crouched low and tiptoed across the deck. A strip of light could be seen around the shutter on the galley window and a wisp of smoke curled up from the cooking fire chimney. They listened at the threshold. A slight squeaking sound could be heard from within. Without waiting, Digby wrenched open the door and strode in. For a moment he was dazzled by the light reflecting off the gleaming pots and pans hanging neatly above the polished stove. Everything in the galley sparkled and shone, even the logs for the fire had been polished. Sitting at the table busily putting an extra shine on a toasting fork was Prudence.

'Oh, Digby,' she cried. 'I thought you'd never get here. I am completely out of things to clean.'

'Ssssssh,' Digby hissed then silenced Prue with a kiss. The others were at the doorway watching the pirate crew, several stirred sufficiently on hearing Prue's voice to sound the alarm. Brains befuddled, they blundered into life and advanced on the hatch. Norm, Dig and Ben drew their daggers; there had been no room for cutlasses in the barrels. Peter Penworthy stood shoulder to shoulder with them in the entrance. He had a cutlass and knew which end was for holding and which end was for poking. That was the extent of his fighting skills but this was no time to draw up a writ or a restraining order. Bravely he waggled his sword at the oncoming hoard but secretly he wished it was a pen.

The ugly mob advanced. Everyone is entitled to be ugly but this lot abused the privilege. Ugly words were uttered by ugly mouths and ugly threats accompanied them. For all that, the pirate crew were reluctant to do more. Many had hangovers, others were still having difficulty focussing, a few had not yet managed to get to their feet but they still yelled abuse and encouragement in a loud and incoherent manner.

They were armed to the eyebrows which, in technical terms, is more highly armed than being armed to the teeth. This was mostly because not many of them had a full set of teeth due to the frequency of fighting and the calcium dissolving qualities of grog and cola.

Ben took a menacing step forward. The leading seamen recoiled. It looked as though, with a little bluff and bluster, the rescuers could make a break for it. Then the increasingly horrible Horatio Hogwash strode on deck and took command.

Battle

Captain Horatio Hogwash took charge. 'Charge!' he yelled and, as one, his murderous crew shuffled forward.

'Charge!' yelled Captain Lloyd and his crew leapt into action. They weren't hardened fighting men like the pirate crew but, being bankers, they certainly knew how to charge. With a cry fierce enough to freeze the assets of any adversary, they made an advance on the Black Pig. It's true they were mostly pen pushers but they had sharpened their quills until they were mightier than the sword.

They crossed the intervening space in three waves. The first was led by Captain Ali. He, with the aid of Nicky Neason and his merry band of fund managers, swung from ropes and deposited themselves on the pirate deck. They were soon dealing recklessly with the befuddled brigands.

Colin and Charley had constructed crossovers which they used to bridge the gap and the second wave of clerks foreclosed on the Black Pig and set about the pirates with punitive interest. Among these, Sally Swift sallied forth, her dagger in one hand and cutlass in the other. She carved her way, laying out pirates left and right. A junior clerk followed behind, gleefully stamping 'account closed' on the foreheads of all her victims.

Other tellers attacked with blood curdling cries of, 'insufficient funds' and 'next window please.' The pirates tried to make a withdrawal but, finding themselves cut off, they were soon looking for a hole in the wall to hide in.

Captain Lloyd commanded the third wave These were the bank's reserves and consisted of mostly the Juniors from customer relations. They stayed on the deck of the Black Horse and called encouragement with cries of coo-eee and yoo-hoo whilst waving constantly. That is why they were called the third wave.

There was however a strong contingent of the most solvent brigands between Prudence's rescue party and the bankers boarding party.

'I think it's time we got out of here,' said Norman, eyeing the line of cutlass toting tyrants that Hogwash was urging forward.

'Just give me a minute, there's something I must do,' said Prudence and she disappeared into the galley before anyone could stop her.

Not daring to take their eyes of the weaving blades of their opponents, the boys could do nothing but brandish their daggers and grimace aggressively until she returned.

'Right, let's go,' she said and charged the pirates. Wielding a broom with devastating effect, she swept the pirates aside. The boys on her flanks made short work of the disarrayed do-badders and they were making good progress until Captain Hogwash sliced the handle of her broom in two. She managed to give him the brush off with the stump of her household implement but he, not wishing to face another brush with the fired-up woman, slipped away before any of them could close in on him.

From the pocket of Prue's apron came a loud ringing sound.

'Quick,' she said. 'Get everyone back on board the Black Horse.'

'Retreat!' shouted Digby to Norman.

'Get back!' shouted Norman to Ben.

'Recoil!' shouted Ben to Captain Ali who met Sally as their forces combined.

'Withdraw!' shouted Ali and Sally to their troops and they all rushed back across the bridges. Some of the pirates tried to follow but were repulsed by Captain Lloyd's reserves that set about them with their handbags. Once all bankers were safely back and a dozen position-closed signs lined the rails, Digby took Prudence in his arms and hugged her.

'Are you alright?' he enquired.

'I'm fine,' she said. 'but it is a shame that their kitchen is so messy.'

'But it was spotless,' said Digby.

'Not for long.' Prudence fished in her pocket and pulled out an oven timer and looked at its dial. 'Any minute now.'

'A mighty explosion rocked the Black Pig. Flames and smoke billowed from its galley windows. The pirates who were all headed there for a soothing cup of tea after the battle were knocked backwards and covered in soot.

'So that's why you insisted we get off their ship.'

'I had already made a batch of cakes using Ben's new recipe with a little embellishment of my own, gun powder sprinkles. I put them in the oven when I popped back to get my broom. It was just a matter of waiting until the stove got to the right temperature.'

'Hell hath no fury like a woman scorned' said Digby with a grin.

Just the Ticket

The crew of the Lexi, with their new member Peter Penworthy, lined the rails to watch the still smouldering Black Pig as it was towed into dry dock for a major refit. Its singed and battered crew had taken board and lodging in the Sticky Seaman.

'I think it is time we left town,' said Norman, stroking his wart.

'I think that can be arranged,' said Captain Ali. 'I hear there is going to be a concert tonight and, if we attend, we may obtain permission to leave on the morning tide.

In that case we will need to lay in some provisions,' said Digby, stroking his left wart. 'How are the funds Norm?'

'We should have enough . . .'

'Oh goody, shopping,' said Prudence. 'Come on, Sal, we will need new dresses and . . .'

'First, we order provisions,' Captain Ali interrupted in an assertive manner adding a belated, 'ahaaar,' to reinforce his authority. 'We will need all the holds to be full; there is no chance of re supply once we leave . . . er, ahaar again.'

'Knobby,' he went on. 'Go to the chandler and order the bulk supplies and get the water tanks refilled. Take young Peter with you. He can draw up a contract to ensure that that chancer of a harbour master doesn't try to rip us off again, aye.'

'Aye aye Cap'n.'

'Ladies, you may get some nice things for the galley if you wish and, if there is anything left over, then a trip to the dress shop can be arranged later.'

'Don't worry ladies,' said Ben, drawing his cutlass and examining its blade. 'I'll go with Knobby and help negotiate the prices.

'Right!' The Captain turned to Norman and Digby. 'Come with me and let's see if we can get invited to the Ball ahaar.'

***

The residence of Governor Peter Piper the Third was a palace in all but name. It spread across a hill at the edge of town like a thick frosting on a cake. The approach was by way of a long, tree lined avenue between the substantial houses of the great and the crooked. The only foot traffic to use this boulevard was from the servants who scurried as inconspicuously as possible along its sides to carry out their duties. The residents always went by carriage.

In echelon formation, the three representatives of the Lexi strode down the centre of the road. Each wore their best clothes. Such a colourful sight they were, Digby in his bright yellow to the left and Norman in a conservative red plus fours suit to the right and Captain Ali in Blue and white taking point. It was a warm day and, by the time they reached the enormous gates, trickles of sweat had made little dark trails down Captain Ali's face from his newly dyed hair.

Puffing slightly from the long uphill walk, he pulled on the large golden bell pull.

'Yeow,' came a yell from somewhere inside. They waited patiently, peering through the gate for some sign of movement. Beyond the ivory and gold bars was a large pink tiled courtyard beyond which was a colonnaded façade in dazzling white with gold piping. Even the small guardhouse that served the main gate was decorated with gold trim.

'I didn't hear a bell,' said Norman. 'Try again.' The Captain gave a couple of hefty pulls.

'Yeow, ow, ow,' it came from the gatehouse. The three Urlanders grinned at each other. Norman grabbed the handle and pulled vigorously.

The language that issued from the gatehouse was positively obscene. Then another voice called out.

'All right, all right, I'm coming.' The gatehouse door creaked open and a wizen hunchback figure emerged. He was wearing an ornate military style livery that presumably used to be gold and white. Now the gold was dulled to a light brown and the few white bits  that weren't stained were grey. A livid red streak glistened on his tunic below his chin.

He shuffled up to the bars of the gate and fixed Captain Ali with his beady eye. The non-beady eye wandered to and fro, to keep an eye on Norman and Digby.

'What do you want zebra face?' Pink drool appeared in the corner of his wart less face as he spoke.

'Ahem, we have come about the Governors Ball,' said the Captain.

'Oh, it's much better now,' said the gateman and turned to go.

'No wait,' said Digby. 'We want tickets to the Governors Ball. The receding figure stopped as if frozen. After a long pause, they heard a slow intake of breath.

'You actually want to go to the ball?' both his eyes whizzed around in their sockets as if trying to follow the gyrations of two flies at once. 'You wouldn't be having fun with a wizen old doorman, would you?'

'No, no,' said Digby. 'Do we look like we're joking?'

'In that get-up you do actually,' said the doorman. 'Now push off before I call the guards.'

'Now listen here my good man . . .' said the Captain.

'Ding Dong,' the doorman yelled. 'Get on the trumpet and call out the guard, we've got troublemakers here.'

Another scrawny creature appeared at the door of the gatehouse. He was unable to step right outside due to the length of chain which appeared to be secured somewhere inside his trousers. He put a long trumpet to his lips and let out a shrill blast. 'Now you are in trouble,' he said with a grin. Digby could not resist and heaved on the bell pull.

'Yeow . . .' the trumpeter was whisked crotch first back into the gatehouse.

The sound of tramping feet heralded the approaching guardsmen.

'Time we went,' said Norman with alarm. He was about to take to his heels.

'Belay that,' said the Captain 'We'll soon sort this out when a suitably trained military man arrives instead of this dingy dolt.'

'I think we should have it on our toes,' said Norman.

'If we want to go to the Ball we'd better hang on and sort it out now,' said Digby stroking his right wart.

'What's going on here?' the sergeant of the guard appeared leading a troupe of about twenty pale pink uniformed soldiers.

'Trouble makers,' said the wild-eyed gateman. 'That one My-Good-Manned me.' he pointed at Captain Ali.

'And that yellow one pulled my chain.' The scrawny trumpeter had reappeared in the doorway.

'Shut up Ding Dong,' said the sergeant and the gateman together. Digby yanked the bell pull. With another plaintive cry Ding Dong disappeared again.

'Ah, Sergeant.' The Captain stepped up to the gate and saluted. 'I am Captain Ali Anxious of the good ship Lexi, this fine golden gentleman is Sir Digby Dingle, arts editor of the Urland Times and my other companion is Norman Knocker esquire, the famous impresario. We seek to hear for ourselves the talents of your illustrious Governor. Kindly advise him that we wait without.

'Wait without what?' said the sergeant.

'They want tickets to the Ball,' said the gateman behind his hand.

'They wants tickets, does they?' said the sergeant, his brow furrowed. 'Nobody actually wants tickets!' The soldiers, drawn up in two rows behind him, were having difficulty trying not to laugh.

'Silence in the ranks,' barked the sergeant. 'Open the gate Igor.'

'Are you sure about this Stanley?' The gateman fished inside his tunic and produced a large rusty key. The sergeant nodded curtly and drew his sword. His men came to attention and drew theirs.

'Run for it!' said Norman. He was prevented from carrying out his own instructions by the restraining hand of the Captain.

The key grated and heavy tumblers clanked inside the lock. Bolts withdrew from retainers and with a grunt and a heave the gate opened a foot or two.

'Hurry up if you're coming,' said the gatekeeper. 'My dinner's getting cold.'

'Soup is it?' said Norman as he squeezed through the gap.

'Yes, tomato.'

'I thought so.'

Once they were all inside, Sergeant Stanley guided the visitors in between two serried ranks of his men at arms. As they marched off, the clang of the gate being closed and locked behind gave them all a feeling of being trapped.

An Audience

With gentle prodding from the sergeant's sword, Norman, Digby and Captain Ali were shepherded in through a side door to the huge building. Inside they found it was a military barracks. Whereas the outside façade gleamed brilliant white, inside was severely shabby and shabbily severe. The guard's accommodation consisted of a large room with thirty rickety iron cots along two opposing walls and a small partitioned office cum bedroom for the sergeant. The drab paint, where it hadn't peeled off the walls, gave little clue to its original colour and the bare patches, of which there were many, showed signs of severe damp. At the far end, a large wood panelled door peeled its varnish in flakes onto the scuffed wooden floor like dandruff. In the centre of the room was a large table with an assortment of rusty metal cutlery, tin mugs and plates. All were in need of washing.

'Prudence would have a wonderful time here,' said Norman. 'Look at the cobwebs around the windows.'

'Cobwebs?' said Digby, 'I thought they were net curtains.' Both of them were whispering out of the corner of their mouths.

'Now then, Sergeant,' said Captain Ali, 'kindly tell your master we are here and wish an audience.' The sergeant slammed the outer door and proceeded to lock it with another large key and led the way to his office.

***

The sergeant who; having warmed to the little group, insisted they called him Stanley, quickly explained how he could arrange for them to attend the concert scheduled for that night.

'While we wait for the men in white coats . . .' the sergeant was saying when he was interrupted by a little round man wearing rubber gloves and a large apron which dragged on the floor in front of him gathering dust and threatening to trip him up as he bustled along.

'What is going on sergeant?' he demanded. The wagon from the loony bin is outside. I told you I'm not going back there; besides I've got a concert to give tonight. He flapped his arms in panic, eyes darting hither and thither in his chubby red face.'

'Calm down My Lord.' The sergeant tried to sooth the bouncing ball of bewilderment. 'It is for these peacocks here.'

'Oh, I'm sorry gentlemen, I didn't realise; it's just that they are always trying to get rid of me. If it wasn't for my beautiful singing voice I'm sure that they would have locked me up years ago.'

'Thank you, My Lord, I will deal with the wagon. Perhaps you had better get back to the cleaning of the auditorium, there's not much time until the performance.'

'Yes, yes, you are quite right Sergeant, carry on.' The little man bustled out of the office and headed for the big flaky door at the end of the barrack room.

'Who was that?' asked Norman trying his best to hold back a laugh.

'That?' said the sergeant. 'That was his lordship Peter Piper, the Governor of this benighted island and your host for this evening.' They all stared after the receding figure.

'I'll be right back,' said Captain Ali and he dashed after the manic monarch before the sergeant could lift a hand to stop him. Not that Sergeant Stanley did lift a hand. He did lift a shoulder in a sort of half shrug and then return to his paperwork.

Whilst ticking the last remaining boxes on the dusty sheets he outlined his plan to get the crew of the Lexi into the concert. He then courteously escorted them to the barracks door where two men in white coats waited, canvas jackets draped over their arms, long straps trailed onto the floor behind them.

'No need for the strait jackets, gentlemen,' said the sergeant. 'These nutters are quite calm for loonies.' He stepped forward and whispered in the ear of one of the attendants then turned to Norm and Dig. 'Go with

the nice gentlemen, they will take you back to your ship and be ready tonight.

'I think I'd rather walk,' said Digby.

'In this heat,' said Norman. 'Are you mad?'

'Chuck them in the van,' said the sergeant.

The men in white coats were strong and ruthlessly efficient. Muttering things like, 'come along now,' and, 'there's a good boy,' they bundled the protesting Urlanders into the back of a closed horse drawn wagon that was waiting outside.

Ticket to Ride

It was hot in the back of the van with no side windows and only a small mesh grill in one of the rear doors. Norm and Dig were separated from the two attendants by more mesh. Once the wagon got going, a welcome breeze wafted through from the open seating at the front. The boys sat opposite each other on the long benches that lined each side of the wagon.

'I wonder what that sergeant whispered to the driver,' whispered Norman.

'I don't know but I doubt if it was anything good.'

The wagon clattered across the courtyard and out of the gate without having to stop then turned sharply to the right.

'Hey,' Digby yelled. 'This isn't the way to the harbour!' Although they had a limited view, the sea was definitely downhill and the wagon took on a distinctly uphill attitude.

'Hoi, where are you taking us?' Digby pushed his fingers through the mesh and shook it like a caged monkey.

'Be quiet, there's a good gentleman,' said the driver through the corner of his mouth. 'We are taking you back by a circuitous route so as not to attract attention. We cannot do that if you are rattling your cage all the time. People will think you are mad.'

'I think they will have a clue anyway seeing as it says "Ever-Rest Loony Bin" on the side of the van,' muttered Norman.

The wagon gathered speed as it turned sharply downhill.

'Ah, now we must be headed towards the coast,' said Digby, clinging to one of the shackles that adorned the inside of their accommodation.

'Or down into hell,' said Norm, similarly clinging on for the sake of his sanity. They had no breath for anything else as the vehicle rattled and banged round multifarious corners, often bouncing off the walls of buildings in the narrow streets. The co-driver started to turn a handle in a device in front of him, which caused it to let out a wail like a chorus of banshees strangling cats or a set of bagpipes in the grip of a serial killer.

However, it wasn't long before the van shrieked and clattered to a stop and the driver gave a heave on a great lever. The rear doors sprang open and the floor tilted almost vertical, ejecting the battered pair in a heap on the dockside cobbles.

'Hoi . . . You could have just asked us to get out,' shouted Digby, staggering to his feet.

'You're lucky,' said the grinning driver. 'We usually do that over a cliff.' With that, he flicked his whip at the horses and they were off, sparks flying from the hooves, wagon rattling and the siren wailing enthusiastically as they careered away from the harbour.

'Thanks for the lift,' Norman called after the receding white van, 'and so inconspicuous too.'

Feeling bruised and battered, they trudged up the gangplank of the Lexi to find frenzied activity on deck.

'And where the hell have you been?' Sally looked over from where Norman's best suit was hanging from the rigging. She had been beating the dust out of it with a broom and her pretty face was smudged with the resultant debris.

'Well we . . .'

'No time . . .' she snapped, 'tell me later. Both of you get below and get cleaned up. We're going out in half an hour.' She reached out a hand as they hastened to obey, grabbed Norman by the throat and, pulling him to her, gave him a big kiss before sending him on his way.

Across the deck Knobby was standing in a barrel of water, half consumed in grey suds, franticly scrubbing himself, clothes and all. 'There's been a message from the Governor. We are going to a gala, whatever that is.' Bubbles billowed from his mouth as he spoke.

Alongside him, Ben was busy with a hammer and chisel trying to scrape the congealed cheese off his shirtfront, pausing occasionally to taste the odd sample. 'We all have to go, then we will be allowed to leave the island.'

The boys entered the cabin to find Prudence carefully ironing Digby's other yellow suit. She looked up as they came in. 'There's a tub in there, you'll have to share,' she said with a grin, 'and don't get mucky water all over my clean floor.'

In the aft cabin they found soap and towels with clean underwear for each of them hanging from a line strung across the room. It took rather a long time to clean up, what with trying, not altogether successfully, to avoid splashing the decking. Eventually they emerged, gleaming white legs visible below gleaming white shorts, hair slick and squeaky clean, and faces pink from scrubbing, or possibly the close encounter with their buddy's naked bodies.

The girls were both wearing their best frocks and were busy pinning up their hair in a formal style as befit the occasion. Hastily the boys dressed and stood to attention to be inspected. With a little adjustment here and there, they were deemed to pass muster and allowed outside.

On deck, Ben and Knobby were subjected to examination too. Prudence had realised some time ago that, when dealing with a sea-going man in matters of personal hygiene, excess scrutiny only leads to mutiny. In fact, she found that Knobby, although still rather damp, had scrubbed up rather well. With regard to Ben, to whom water is something of an anathema, she felt the swab could do with a good swabbing but he had made the effort, putting his hair into a random assortment of pigtails and most of the cheese from his chest had been transferred to his teeth.

The sound of a siren and the clattering of hooves on cobblestones heralded the return of the van, only this time the drivers had exchanged their white coats for crimson footman's livery

It now had curtains at the windows and a splosh of paint had been daubed over the sign on the side obscuring the "ny Bin" of the lettering.

The coachmen doffed their tricorn hats and bowed low as the party descended the gangplank. Digby led the way and held his hand out for Prudence as she daintily lifted the hem of her long golden skirt and swept elegantly down the ramp. She was followed by Sally who, unused to the volume of blue silk flapping round her legs, scooped it up over one arm revealing and hastily re-covering a large dagger tucked into her garter. She tottered down the slope on ridiculously high heels with Norman close behind, to help steady her descent and keep her decent. Knobby and Ben bowed politely to each other at the top of the gangplank then jostled each other shoulder to shoulder as they struggled to the quayside. With full ceremony, the coachmen assisted their charges into their seats slamming the doors behind them and, with only a single turn on the siren, made a much more sedate ascent to the Governor's palace.

No Business like Show Business

The wagon or "Carriage" as the footmen liked to call it now, rattled its way unhindered through the mansion's gates and drew to a noisy halt in front of the main entrance. A crowd that had gathered, filling the courtyard, were held back by the entire compliment of guards resplendent in their best, only slightly tatty,

uniforms wielding long and vicious looking pikes. Any one pressing too hard was slapped severely around the head with these large wet fish and sent reeling backwards. In truth, there was little interest from the masses to push on into the building as their presence was only due to the fact that it was compulsory on concert days. However, curiosity overcame one or two to see who the celebrities in the van marked "Ever-Rest Loo," were.

The footman hastened to open the back doors but, before he could reach for the handle, the driver pulled his lever and dumped his charges unceremoniously onto the cobbles.

'Sorry . . . force of habit,' he called back with the hint of a smirk.

The crowd roared with laughter but this was quickly subdued by the fish wielding guards.

'You'll feel the force of my fist in a minute,' growled Digby as he helped Prudence up from where she had landed comfortably on top of Ben.

Sally, struggling with the folds of her dress, helped Norman to his feet with her free hand and glared at the driver as her fingers closed on the hilt of her dagger. Norman, judging her mood, placed a gentle restraining hand on her arm giving the coachmen just enough time to make their escape. The party dusted themselves off, recovered what was left of their dignity and assembled in echelon in front of the steps. Digby resplendent in his yellow suit turned and bowed to the audience then led the way to the accompaniment of a ripple of applause, the occasional raspberry and the odd slap of fish on face towards the mansion.

A broad red carpet had been laid up to the grand porticoed entrance and, standing with his back to them on the top landing, was a tall and strangely familiar figure. Resplendent in the blue and gold uniform of an admiral of the fleet complete with sword and buckler, a brass telescope under his arm, Captain Ali turned to greet them.

'Wow, Captain, nice threads,' gasped Norman. 'Where did you get them?'

'They come with my new job, "Temporary Admiral of the Ever-Rest Navy." Follow me.' He led the way into the grand auditorium, which gleamed in the light of a huge chandelier that hung over the tiered seating of the stalls. High at the rear was the curved balcony of the dress circle and, to each side sticking out from the wall like upturned ears, were VIP boxes. Captain/Admiral Ali took them via a back stair and settled them into the plush red velour seats of the guest box. From here they had an excellent view of the stage or would have once the safety curtain was lifted.

The auditorium doors had been opened and the audience began to fill the seats. Apart from the occasional squabble over the seats nearest the exit, they moved with all the resignation of those unable to resign from their task. The sound of fish on fizzog like sporadic clapping mingled with the squeak of poorly lubricated seats and general grumbles from the general population.

'It's a good crowd,' Digby remarked, leaning over to get a better view. His plumed bonnet fluttered gracefully to land in the crowd. 'Oh no, not my hat again.'

'I'll get it,' yelled Sally, leaping for a rope she saw tied to a hook by the side of their box. The hat was bobbing about above the heads of the crowd as it was tossed to and fro.

'Sally, wait,' Norman's warning was too late; she had already unhitched the hitch and was being carried aloft.

He grabbed the tail end as it flicked past and was whisked over the side too. Luckily, their combined weight was enough to counter balance the chandelier that was plummeting downwards towards the packed auditorium.

The crowd cheered, at last they had something to entertain them. The apparition in blue silk swung high above their heads in a sweeping arc. The young man that trailed behind her was almost at the end of his rope. His yells of terror were easily mistaken for a battle cry. They swiftly completed a circuit of the hall and, in the excitement, someone threw Digby's hat high in the air. Whether by luck or design it lodged on Norm's trailing foot. As they zoomed back towards the guest box, Digby reached over the balcony and grabbed at the brim. A ripping sound accompanied the bursting of seams, Digby was further drawn out of the box but Prudence had grabbed his trousers and, with the aid of Ali, dragged him back in. The three of them hauled on Norman then on the rope until they had recovered Sally. It took a while to calm the girl down.

'Again, again, again,' she shrieked. It wasn't until Prudence pointed out that during their aerial exploits the giant chandelier was hovering only inches above the heads of the people in the stalls that she could be persuaded to defer her next flight to another day.

'It doesn't seem to be any the worse for wear.' Digby was examining his precious hat. 'I could have sworn I heard a ripping sound when I grabbed it.'

Prudence settled back in her seat and tilted her head to look behind him. 'I would make sure you hold it behind you the next time you take a bow.' She grinned.

'Oh, that's where the draught is coming from.' Digby joined their laughter and purposefully regained his seat.

'Don't get too comfortable, Prudence,' said Ali, 'you're coming with me.'

On with the Show

The safety curtain made its halting way up to a prolonged fanfare from a line of liveried trumpeters and, with a nervous glance at the retracting canvas, Sergeant Stanley marched to centre stage. A speaking tube rose majestically out of the floor in front of him. He crouched down a little to speak into it.

'My Lords, Ladies and Gentlemen.' His voice boomed out of dozens of cones fixed to the walls of the auditorium. 'It is my pleasure and privilege to introduce, your friend and his, the Monarch formerly known as Governor Peter Piper.'

To the sound of another fanfare the sergeant bowed low and backed off the stage as his ruler bounced out into the spotlight. His arrival triggered an outburst of boos which were quickly drowned out by the applause-like sound of fish on heads followed by half-hearted cheers and clapping.

Ignoring the speaking tube he spoke through a megaphone.

'Friends . . .'

'Boo . . . slap. . .'

'Friends, Everestians, Countrymen, lend me your ears.'

'You can have them if I don't have to listen . . . slap . . . ouch.'

'I come not to bury music but to save it.' A hush descended over the theatre as his words rang out.

'I declare the ban on music lifted and, to encourage the rise of new talent, there will be an annual competition to find the best entertainers in the land.

'For this, the inaugural "Everest's got the Y-factor," I have enlisted the aid of some specialist judges.' He gestured with a sweep of his hand towards the box where the Urlanders were seated. 'Sir Digby Dingle, arts editor of the Urland Times, Norman Knocker esquire, the famous impresario and Sally Swift, well known dizzy person and pretty face.' He bowed low in their direction. The trio in the box stood and bowed back, first to the Governor then to the crowd who were by now clapping and cheering voluntarily.

'The contestants have been dragged here from the prison for the vocally incontinent and have been pardoned from their crimes against my eardrums.' A cross between a chorus line and a chain gang shuffled onto the stage behind him. The crowd roared as they recognised some of their favourite street singers, many of whom they hadn't seen or, more importantly, heard from in years.

'And so, without more ado . . . remove their restraints and let the show commence.' Governor Peter left the stage to tumultuous applause. The bemused entertainers held out their hands so that their guards could remove their shackles, the trumpeters joined the band that had previously been hiding in the pit and began to play and, for the first time in a decade, the people of Eve-Rest heard music that wasn't ruined by the voice of their monarch.

Governor Peter joined Ali and Prudence in the Royal Box.

'How do you think it went Admiral?'

'Excellent, Sire. Guaranteed box office.'

'And you my dear, did you think I looked splendid in the spotlight?' He patted Prue's knee solicitously.'

'You were magnificent My Lord,' she replied, inching a little further away.

'Don't you think I should give them a song?' The monarch started to get up.

'Oh, no . . .' Ali and Prudence almost shouted in unison.

'Let them enjoy themselves a bit longer,' muttered Prudence. The Governor turned and glared at her.

'What she means,' said Ali, 'you are too hard an act to follow.'

'Oh . . . yes I am, aren't I . . .? Perhaps at the end then.'

The concert got underway and after each act the spotlight was turned onto the judges who did their best to be puerile, condescending and ill informed.

At the end a winner was declared and, to tumultuous applause, the Governor presented him with a year's supply of earplugs.

'And now,' he said, 'how would you like to join me in a little duet?'

The unfortunate winner hung his head and held out his hands to accept the chains as Peter turned to the front to find the last of his audience bringing up the rear of a stampede towards the exit.

All that remained was a pile of badly damaged pike in the front row.

'Fish and chips anyone?' said the Governor.

Free at last Free at Last.

As honoured guests, the judges could not be excused from the back-stage banquet and, as the pike had to be filleted and fried, the Governor entertained them with a recital of his greatest hits over drinks in the green room. Ever resourceful, Norman managed to turn it into a sing along to help mitigate the pain. After copious quantities of strong beverages they were soon all rolling out the barrel with gusto by the time the fish and chip supper arrived.

In the meantime, having obtained the necessary permit to go to sea, Captain Ali, Ben and Knobby contrived a swift exit to make their way back to the Lexi to prepare it for departure. With a quick call into the harbour office to make himself a nuisance for just long enough for the harbour master to be glad to see the back of them, Ali soon had the promise of fresh provisions and casks of water for delivery first thing in the morning.

Before going to bed, Ben joined Peter who, having won the toss, had remained on board as night watchman. For an hour or so they sorted out the bins in the hold ready for the delivery. Almost all had been cleared out already and just needed the last bits of debris swept up. Cargo bin "S" was the one bin that remained full. Someone had considerately stuck a label on it saying, "DANGER Brussels Sprouts Emergency Use Only." He would have cleared it out to make room for more delectable comestibles but, such was his aversion to the little green spawn of the devil, he gave it a wide berth. Consequently, the sibilations of the ever-shifting contents never attracted his attention.

Meanwhile, Knobby climbed to the top of the mast to renew his relationship with the crows that nested there and was pleased to be introduced, in raucous fashion, to the newly hatched additions to the lookout crew. It was no surprise that these birds had managed to find a suitably productive way to pass the time during their period in port.

While he was there he took the opportunity to give a powerful blast on the Sailors' whistle. He heard nothing of course, but sensitive ears all over Ever-Rest pricked up and those for whom it was more significant, immediately prepared to meet the summons.

Phd was first to react. Still with exotic blossoms in her hair, she cajoled her temporary mate out of their arboreal nest and set him the task of organising a leaving party. It would start at dawn and run all day. The sound of their revelry would echo around the forests and peaks of the island far into the following night.

***

Captain Ali was concerned. He sat in the wheelhouse of the Lexi with the harbour charts set out in front of him. He had no worries about navigating the long fjord under the guns of the harbour defences as he was told that, if he flew a red flag, he would be allowed to pass unmolested. Besides, he was an Admiral of the Ever-Rest Navy now so should be able to command whatever he wanted. No, that wasn't his fear. It was the activity on the far side of the harbour that held his apprehensive attention.

The Black Pig, still largely blackened by fire and smoke, was under repair. Somehow, Captain Horatio Hogwash had cajoled the dockyard shipwrights to work round the clock to restore the pirate vessel to fighting fitness. He had sworn revenge on Captain Ali and all his crew. The accountant in Ali's head calculated that their arch-enemy would not be caught out again by Ben Kipling's exceedingly rocky hotcakes.

No doubt, if Hogwash managed to leave the harbour first, he would be laying in wait for the departing postal vessel with murder on his bloodthirsty mind. The sound of hammering and sawing continued to disturb Ali's rest all night. With his head buried in his pillows and the cabin doors and windows closed against the din, it was still four am when he finally managed to nod off.

At ten past four the Captain's cabin door burst open and in rolled Digby.

'Wha' y'doin' in bed already?' he yelled, arms waving in all directions. 'The night is still young.' At this point the young Urlander made a rapid transition from "ready to party forever," to "comatosed," and collapsed in a somnolent heap on the floor. Norman followed him in, only to trip over the insensible carcass's and find he was incapable of rising. The girls were of no help either. They just stood there cross-legged and giggling.

'Knobby . . .' Ali roared, 'Get these lubbers out of here!'

Bleary eyed, the cabin boy made his way into the room and grabbed the first pair of legs he could lay his hands on. 'What shall I do with them, Cap'n?'

'I don't know . . . throw them in irons.'

Knobby started to heave, only to realise he had one leg from each of them and they wouldn't go through the doorway side by side. He stopped, scratched his head and said, 'We haven't got any irons Cap'n.'

'I know,' snapped Captain Ali. 'Take them to their rooms.'

Ben arrived to see what all the fuss was about, the hem of his red flannel nightshirt dragging along the ground as he walked. 'Wha . . .'

'Give me a hand, Ben,' Knobby puffed.

Between them they dragged the boys to the appropriate cabin and left them to be ineptly ministered to by their female partners. After further bouts of giggling, several percussions of heads on floorboards, furniture and what have you, the Lexi finally fell silent. Only the distant sound of carpentry disturbed the sleeping harbour.

***

The first of the supplies arrived at dawn and, with unprecedented reluctance, Norm and Dig joined the dockers in the task of stowing the sacks, barrels, crates and chests in the appropriate alphabetical storage bins. Befuddled of mind and churnupled of stomach, Digby toiled inattentively whereas Norman, in equal measure, was churnupled of mind and befuddled of stomach as he inattentively toiled. Quite confusing really and indeed they were.

Prudence and Sally were similarly indisposed so breakfast was late and a rather slapdash affair. Ben, as usual, covered the table with the volcanic ash of his enthusiastically consumed cheese toastie. Prudence started to scold him and took a cursory swipe at the debris with a cleaning cloth but her heart wasn't in it.

'Never again,' she kept saying, 'never again,' until all the crew were served then she crept away to find a dark corner of her cabin to curl up in.

Fortified by a hearty meal, the goods were stowed in more or less alphabetical order but it was nightfall before the task was accomplished. With clearer heads the evening meal was consumed with much more relish than had breakfast and it was early to bed for all of them. All they needed was the Sailors and they could set sail for home.

Captain Ali fell sound asleep as soon as he became horizontal but woke with a start a few hours later. Something had roused him but as he lay there he couldn't figure out what it was. The ship rocked on its moorings, the ropes binding it to the harbour wall creaked softly in a steady regularity. Knobby snored in perfect syncopation with their rhythm. The harbour and town slept peacefully around them.

That was it! Ali leapt to his feet. The banging and sawing that had lulled him into the land of nod had stopped. Captain Hogwash must have completed his repairs. Pausing only to grab his hat Ali rushed on deck. His long-johns bleached to within an inch of their lives by Sally were almost luminous in the light of the equatorial full moon. By their glow he found Ben dozing in the wheelhouse.

'Wake up, yer lily livered . . .' Ali yelled.

'Wha' . . .' The old sea dog fumbled a shaky salute, 'All's quiet, Cap'n.'

'That's the trouble.' Ali grabbed Ben by his cheese encrusted lapel and wished he hadn't. 'You're supposed to be on watch . . . Where's the Black Pig?' He ran to the rail dragging the ever-confused Ben with him and peered across the harbour towards the dry dock. To his relief the masts of the pirate ship were still there swaying gently from side to side. 'Look,' Captain Ali hissed, 'they've flooded the dock. She must be seaworthy.'

'Aye, Cap'n, they can be at sea by dawn . . . Good riddance I say.'

'That means they can lay in wait for us outside the harbour.'

'Not so, Mon Capitan.' Ben was at last getting his head together. "Once outside the protection of the fjord they will have to sail west else be swept away by the fierce currents.'

'They could always drop anchor.' Ali stroked his wart. 'With a fair wind the Black Pig is much faster than the Lexi. We need to get underway as soon as possible.'

'But we can't move without the Sailors. Knobby put the call out last night. I hope they heard it.'

'Get him out of bed, Ben. He can give them another blast.'

'Knobby arrived barefoot and bleary. 'Wassup . . . er, Capon,' he mumbled, rubbing his eyes.

'The Black Pig's ready for sea, get up the mast and call the Sailors again.'

'But the crows won't like it.'

'Stone the crows! They can keep watch. Its time they earned their corn,

'It's maize, Sir.'

'What?'

'I feeds em maize, Cap'n, not corn.

Well take some with you. Now get up the mast.'

'Aye-aye, Sir,' Knobby tucked his nightshirt into his pants, grabbed the whistle and started to climb.

Ben came back on deck munching on a chunk of cheese. 'Give it three blasts, Knobby, that's the emergency recall.' He shouted, spraying the base of the mast with the remnants of his mouthful.

With the signal sent and the birds circling and alert there was nothing more they could do. Knobby and the Captain settled down in the wheelhouse for the remainder of the brief night but sleep did not come easy for Ali. He was quite relieved when the first glow of the golden dawn touched the tips of the surrounding mountains.

Ready or Not, Here we Come.

The gleaming line of sunshine had barely put a slice of gold along the tops of the buildings in the town when the distant rumble of the approaching Sailors reached their ears. The crew were all up enjoying breakfast in the galley. The talk was about where they should go next. Digby was all for heading east to complete the circumnavigation of the globe but Ali was against it.

'From what I've been told,' he declared, 'no ship that left Ever-Rest in that direction ever returned.'

'You can hardly blame them for that,' said Digby. 'Would you want to come back here, the way they treated you.'

'You have a point,' said Norm, 'but that was before. It's a lot better now music is allowed.'

'The fact remains that to the east lays the waterfall at the edge of the world,' said Ali.

'That's a fact we set out to disprove, right.' Digby reminded them.

'Or prove,' said Norm, stroking his wart. 'Then where would we be?'

'Well, the water must go somewhere,' said Digby.

'Yep, down,' said Ben.

'To where?' Ali waggled a finger at them.

'All the way, I suppose.' Digby grinned.

Exasperated and frustrated Ali stormed out.

'Now boys, play nice.' Prudence started clearing up. 'I think it's time we headed for home, east or west doesn't matter. Isn't Urland to the north anyway?'

'She's right, northeast it is,' said Digby.

The sound of the approaching Sailors had become a rhythmic tramp tramp of leathery prehensile feet on pavement, so they all trooped on deck to welcome the return of their faithful rowers.

Out in the harbour the coastguard cutter was cutting through the water towards the open gates of the dry dock. Even from where the Lexi was moored it was obvious by the activity on the deck of the Black Pig they were making ready to depart.

'So it's a race is it, ahar. Stand by all hands, let's get the Lexi shipshape,' shouted Ali. 'We push off as soon as the Sailors arrive. The *ahar* was involuntary.

'I thought the Lexi was already the shape of a ship,' said Prudence with a laugh.

'Make sure all the cargo is lashed down, this is going to be a bumpy ride whichever way we head.' Captain Ali sprang onto the poop deck. The apes are close. I can see their dust.'

'If they are dusty make them wipe their feet, said Prudence. 'I've just washed the decks.'

'Ok,' laughed Digby. 'Perhaps you'd better start baking some ammunition, just in case.'

'Coming up,' she said as she headed for the galley.

'And Prue . . .' Ben called after her, 'you'd better burn them.'

'Burn them! You mean on purpose?' She shrugged and disappeared inside.

Fjord Race

With much hooing and heeing, the Sailors clambered aboard the Lexi. Phd led the way, a new and even more exotic flower in her hair. She greeted the Urlanders with hugs and hairy faced kisses.

'Ben, explain our situation will you.' Ali wheezed as he stooped on the poop to retrieve his hat that had been knocked off by Phd's embrace. Her clasp had squeezed all his breath away.

'Ay-ay, Cap'n.' Ben turned to the enthusiastic seven-foot green ape-lady, 'hoo hoo eee,' he squealed and went on to explain with his limited ape vocabulary the need for a hasty departure.

She responded with shrieks of her own that galvanised the other Sailors into action. Many of them had leapt over the side to freshen up from their long dust journey but they swarmed back in response to the urgent calls of their leader.

'Cap'n,' Knobby called from the crows-nest where he was keeping a lookout and avoiding the exuberance of Phd, 'The Pilot boat is towing the Black Pig out into the Fjord.'

Within ten minutes the Sailors were all seated at their oars and the last loose items were all stowed away. In the galley Sally was helping Prudence whisk up a couple of batches of batter for the cakes with which they hoped to batter the pirate ship.

The pirate ship had already crossed to the harbour entrance by the time the Lexi was pushed away from the harbour wall. With Knobby at the wheel, the rowers pulled strongly and they gained quickly on the Black Pig which was being towed with only half the Sailor power.

Ben called encouragement to the rowing teams with shouts of 'Hee Ho'.

Norman called encouragement with shouts of Heave Ho.

Digby shouted encouragement with calls of, 'In, Out', getting faster as they gained speed.

Phd stood next to the Captain on the forecastle and hee'd and hoo'd as well.

'Just a minute,' said Captain Ali 'shouldn't you be down there rowing?' He looked back onto the rowing deck. All the sweeps were manned, well aped anyway.

It seemed they had picked up a substitute. There was no time for an explanation so, for the moment, he let it drop and went back to worrying about how to get in front of his archenemy Horatio Hogwash. 'If we don't get in front where the fjord opens out to the harbour lagoon there will be no way to pass in the narrows.'

Phd seemed to understand. With a nod of her huge hairy green head she ran down to the rowing deck, the better to encourage her shipmates.

The Lexi shot across the dock with unprecedented speed violating all navigational regulations. Even so, the Black Pig was well out into the loch by the time they cleared the harbour mouth. As momentum built up they started to overhaul the enemy but would they make it past before they reached the narrows? Anxious was anxious, Ali worried about the race, allied to the fact that the rock cakes would not be done in time to fight off a pirate attack once they left the protected waters of Ever-rest. Confident that even horrible Horatio Hogwash would not try anything while under the guns that lined the fjord, their only hope was to get past and show the brigands a clean pair of heels in the open sea. Clean heels would be a foregone conclusion with Prudence in charge of the laundry. Also, once the Black Pig was released from its tow, their square-rigged sails were at the mercy of the wind so the Lexi would row away directly to windward. The best the Black Pig could do was tack after them. *Ahar*, he thought.

They were close behind their adversary now but the rocks on either side were getting closer. One chance.

'Take her past to starboard,' Ali yelled to Knobby.

'Three points to starboard it is Sir.' Knobby eased the wheel over.

'Full speed ahead,' Ali yelled to Ben.

'What ye think we're doing already?' said Ben. But hoo'd at the Sailors anyway.

'Faster,' said Ali.

'They canny take any more Cap'n,' Ben replied.

Their bow was just about alongside the Black Pig's stern. Ali could see the glint in Hogwash's eye. The varlet shook his fist at them. Ali made a smart salute. Hogwash pushed his swarthy helmsman away from the wheel of his craft and swung it hard over. The ship slewed to the side, catching the Lexi's bowsprit a glancing blow, turning them towards the ever-closer rocks. Knobby compensated by swinging the wheel the other way but the precipitous sheer walls were already towering above them. It was Phd's timely command that saved them from grinding into the granite. The port oars hauled in reverse and they swung away. Even so, the starboard sweeps had to be rapidly drawn in to prevent them from being dashed against the fjord wall. They had lost a lot of their momentum and could only watch as the Black Pig slid into the narrows, safe from any chance of an overtake.

Once safely back on course, Ali told the rowers to ease back and save their strength for when they emerged. The break for the open sea would be a challenging one.

Knobby scaled the mast again to keep an eye on the now receding pirate ship leaving Ali at the wheel. Prue's first batch of rock cakes was safely in the oven while Norm and Dig set up the cannon.

With a certain amount of translation difficulty, Ben made enquiries into the inclusion of the additional

Sailor and reported back to the Captain. 'Ahem . . .' he began, ahem, er, ahem, Captain. It appears that there were certain events ashore while we were in Ever-rest, Cap'n.'

'I am aware of that. We had quite a time didn't we?'

Aye, well, . . . while we were having quite a time in the port, our Sailors were having quite a time in the hills, ahar.'

'Aye, they're known for their parties.'

Well in this case, the party of the first part, Phd, met the party of the second part, our new Sailor. Roger, that's his name.'

'How nice,' said Captain Ali, rapidly losing interest.

'Well they fell in love and were married. These things happen fast in ape society, ahar.'

'Well as long as he pulls his weight that's no problem if he comes along.'

'Ah, that's so romantic.' Sally, who had been cooling off in the galley doorway overheard the conversation. She called back to Prudence who was prudently preparing more cake-mix. 'Did you hear that? Phd got married.'

'How wonderful.' Prue came to the door, wiping her hands and, together they hurried over to embrace their ape friend.

'And there's more,' said Ben to Ali in a lowered voice. It seems that Roger has lived up to his name, ahar.'

'And?'

'Well we can look forward to the patter of huge hairy feet in the spring, ahar.'

'Oh . . . Let's hope we are all safely back in Urland by then, shall we?' The captain stared ahead but a wistful smile flickered momentarily on his moustachioed lips.

'Ahoy below,' Knobby called from his lofty perch. 'The pilot boat has slipped its cable and is rowing back. The Black Pig is under sail now.'

'Keep an eye on them Knobby,' said the Captain.

'Eye-eye.' said Knobby.

Hope of a Dash Dashed

The Black Pig had disappeared round the headland to the north. It was the only way any sensible seaman would head as to the south lay Uverland. It's dark foreboding presence under the depressing red sun always brought great trepidation to seafarers.

'We should turn south,' said Digby. 'Hogwash will be laying in wait to the north.'

'But what about the great trepidation?' said Norm.

'It's time to be intrepid,' said Digby.

Let's take it to-em, said Sally, as she sharpened a large kitchen knife. 'We have plenty of ammunition in the oven already.'

'Whatever you decide,' said Prue, 'but I don't want to have to clean the Black Pig's kitchen again. It was disgusting euk . . . ahar, etcetera.' Neither girl was in a mood for any nonsense.

Captain Ali zigzagged the little craft in the mouth of the fjord. The top of a mast bearing skull and crossbones was just visible above the headland.

'I've heard tales . . .' Ben began.

Ali swung the wheel, turning the ship decisively to the south. The whole crew looked at him open mouthed at the arbitrary decision.

'Anything is better than another one of Ben's nautical anecdotes,' Ali shrugged. All but one of our bold travellers had to agree.

'They've unfurled sails.' Knobby could see over the rocks from his vantage point. 'They intend to give chase.'

'Full speed on the sweeps,' Ali called out. 'Our only chance is to clear the lee of Ever-rest before they can catch us.'

Behind the island was a long vee of slack water before the fierce current would take hold and sweep any craft towards the waterfall at the edge of the world. The Lexi was propelled across the widest part with every sinew of the rowing team's formidable strength but the pursuing sailing craft used the strong wind that swirled around the obstructing mountains and was gaining fast.

'Ok Prue, it's time to burn some cakes,' said Digby. 'Stand by the cannon, Norm.'

Powder was loaded, cakes were put in the hottest part of the oven and reserve supplies of batter mixed; but time was running out. The Black Pig, brimming with barbaric brigands, bent on battle, was bearing down on them. Would the cakes be burnt in time?

'They're coming along side Cap'n,' Knobby called from the crows-nest.

'Where's my ammunition?' Captain Ali called to the galley of the galley.

'Just coming Ali,' called Sally from the galley of the galley.

'One minute,' put in Prue as Sally appeared with the tray of smoking lumps of rock-cakes. 'Sprinkle these on them before you load up but fire straight away. She handed Sally a small dish of what looked like hundreds and thousands but in fact was only about a hundred. Sally dashed onto the poop deck, Norm and Peter loaded half of her tray-full into the cannon and Digby sighted along the barrel. The pirate ship was so close he could hardly miss. The huge sails were billowing above the decks where the pirates, cutthroats with cutlasses every one, crouched on deck. Some had grapnels swinging from ropes ready to throw and hook onto the Lexi. If they could lock the two craft together, our intrepid explorers would be overwhelmed by their superior numbers in no time.

Digby touched his taper to the fuse on the gun. All the pirates ducked down. They knew what was coming, or did they? With a roar and a cloud of smoke the cannon went off. A shower of projectiles was propelled into the air, not at the pirates but at the sails.

They struck the canvas, some passing right through while others splatted themselves against the tough cloth and started to slide down in smouldering streaks.

'The cakes were not hot enough, Prue.' Norm shouted. The pirate ship continued to move up alongside. The pirates could be seen laughing at them.

'Give it a minute,' Prudence was leaning on the galley door post wiping her hands on a tea towel, the hint of a smile on her lips.

Suddenly the burnt cake residue that still resided on the sails sparkled then sprang to life. Flames danced across the canvas wherever the crumbs clung. The stuff that had fallen, apparently harmlessly, to the deck suddenly started popping and spitting setting the pirates hopping and skipping and, in some cases, smoking. The pirate ship lost some way as the sails began to blaze.

'Quick,' said Digby, 'reload.' The gun crew sprang into action again.

The rowers pulled harder encouraged by Phd and Ben. Captain Ali turned the wheel away from the pursuing pirate craft but there was little room to manoeuvre as they were close to the headland.

Digby sighted the cannon and touched off the fuse but, just as he did so, the Lexi lurched sideways and rolled onto its side, caught in a fierce current. They had come out of the protected waters. The cannon was tilted up sending its charge almost straight up in the air. The Lexi careened across the bows of the Black Pig and Captain Hogwash had no choice but to turn away. Seeing how the Lexi was caught by the tide, Hogwash continued to turn left into the safety of the slack water only to find that the discharge from the cannon

showered down on them, quickly destroying what remained of his sails.

Not having any oars, the pirate ship was helpless and soon drifted into the grip of the mighty current and was whisked away towards the waterfall at the edge of the world.

Meanwhile Captain Ali regained control of his craft. Although it rolled and pitched he managed to point their bows into the current and the all but exhausted rowers managed to stem their progress toward the receding pirate ship. They couldn't keep this up for long. A new battle had begun, this time against the force of nature and it was one they were slowly losing.

Waterfall at the Edge of the World

Despite all the efforts of the Sailors and Captain Ali's determination at the wheel, they could not get back into the protection of the island and were being swept sideways towards the edge of the world. Phd had joined the rowers, allowing them one at a time to take a break and get some food. However, the current was too strong for them to drop over the side to forage for seaweed as they normally would and had to satisfy themselves with whatever vegetables were in the storage bins.

Realising that it was hopeless, Ali allowed the little craft to drift with the rowers taking it easy to recover their strength but he realised that the only course he could steer was to the south. The giant red sun was rising ahead of them turning the sky purple and the sea the colour of blood. They were heading towards the mysterious southern continent.

'I don't like the look of the sky,' Digby said, staring to the south.

'It's better than to the east.' Norm joined them on the bridge and they all looked in that direction. Heavy clouds tumbled and rolled around the sky illuminated by frequent flashes of lightning. The sea on the horizon looked angry. It rose and fell, spitting and boiling. It seemed to be in conflict with the sky above and very bad tempered indeed.

'I'll rest the rowers as much as possible today but by tomorrow we will be in amongst that and need all their strength again.' Ali looked back to the south, 'unless we make landfall in Uverland.'

'The Land of Dark Foreboding.' Norm shivered.

'At least we are better off than Captain Hogwash and his crew,' said Digby. They could just make out the pitiful remnants of the Black Pig's sails flapping uselessly on its mast as it was being drawn remorselessly to its doom.

'By the way,' said Captain Ali, 'that was a good idea shooting their sails, young Digby. How did you know the cakes would turn into fireworks?'

'I didn't. It was just that you could take someone's eye out with them cakes if you fired straight at them.'

'It was them sprinkles Prue had us add, wasn't it? What was it? gunpowder?'

'Yes, sealed in hard icing,' said Prudence.

'Well done everyone, anyway,' said Ali.

'I hope they manage to escape the waterfall,' said Prue. 'There is a strong wind.'

***

Although they rowed steadily south and the red orb of Leviathan rose higher in the sky before dipping briefly down again to mark the passing of another day, they were drawn ever closer to the troubled eastern horizon. Except that it was not a horizon any more, it was an imminent and fuming storm the like of which had rarely been survived at sea.

While the rowers took a break to feed again, Sally came around with mugs of hot tea.

'Better tell Prue to put out the galley fire and batten down all the lose articles. This is going to get rough,' said Ali, swaying in time with the roll of the ship and keeping what remained of his tea in the mug.

'She's already doing it,' Sally replied. 'Peter is doing the same in the hold.'

'Good. Norm and Dig, you stay with me to help with the wheel. Ben, you get yourself down to encourage the Sailors.

'I'll just climb up and secure the crow's nest,' said Knobby. 'I can stand lookout from up there.'

'Nay lad,' said Ben. 'Ye'll be washed away when the first squall hits.'

'I'll be fine if I lash myself to the masthead and the crows will be less frightened if I'm up there with them.' And with that, he was gone, shinning up the pole like a monkey.

The sea rushed the Lexi relentlessly towards the steamy cloud that obscured the fate that awaited them. The ship rolled in the increasing swell and the mist rolled over them, damp and warm condensing on the rigging. It settled on the Sailors' green fur making them shimmer and glisten as they bent in perfect unison to their task. They rowed steadily to keep the rudder effective but, despite Ali's efforts to steer away, everyone knew they were caught in the current's unrelenting grip.

Phd gripped the pulpit rail and leaned over the bow to peer ahead. The crew gathered around the Captain, drawn by the distant whistling sound.

Prudence wiped the compass binnacle again. 'What is it?' she asked nervously. 'It sounds like a kettle boiling.'

'More like a hundred kettles,' said Norman, stroking his wart.

'Maybe thousands,' said Peter, ominously.

'I think the mist is clearing.' Knobby's disembodied voice drifted down from the crow's-nest. 'Yes, we'll be out of it soon. You'd better get a hold of something, it looks rough out there.'

Suddenly, as if coming out from under a duvet, the Lexi emerged from the cloud and the waterfall was revealed.

.

Phd has a plan

Above them the sky was grey with ominous rolling clouds. Threatening though they were, this did not hold their attention because ahead, across the rushing tumbling ocean, the waterfall at the edge of the world crossed their line of travel. Like a hump in water it curved away from them on both sides. Beyond was a vast void and beyond that a smoking column that rose dramatically, feeding the clouds high above.

Ali swung the wheel away from their impending doom but all it did was pirouette the craft without changing their direction of travel.

'More power!' he yelled to Ben.

Hoarsely, Ben ee'd and hoo'd at the rowers.

Phd shrieked more of their language and waved her great long arms frantically. The rowers stopped rowing in response.

'Phd, what're you doing?' Captain Ali yelled.

The great ape gestured to the Captain as if turning the wheel.

'It's hard over already!' he shouted. The Lexi continued its pirouettes.

Gesticulating wildly, Phd rapidly made her way back to the wheelhouse.

'She doesn't look a happy bunny,' said Norman.

'I'm not a happy bunny', said the Captain. 'Don't let her in boys.'

Norm, Dig and Peter obediently barred the door. Peter drew his dagger and held it in front of him with a shaky hand.

Looking decidedly un-bunny-like Phd loomed over them. 'For goodness sake,' her voice boomed through the little cabin, 'do what I say or we'll all be killed.'

Slack jawed and frozen to the spot they looked at her until Peter's dagger clattered to the floor.

'W - what, did you say?' Ali stammered.

'No time to explain, give me the wheel.' Phd brushed past the boys like they were a bead curtain.

'I'm the Captain . . .' Ali's voice trailed off.

'Let her do it,' Prudence called as she backed into the arms of the bewildered Digby. 'She's more to lose than any of us.'

'Sally likewise clung to Norman as the Lexi spiralled ever more rapidly towards the abyss.

Phd placed her great hairy hand on the wheel and Ali meekly withdrew to one side. The wheel spun first this way, then that under the control of the ape. She called in firm but calm tones to her compatriots on the oars.

They started to row, steadily at first but with increasing power. The Lexi stopped its spinning and settled on a straight course.

'She's driving us straight at the edge,' Sally called in alarm.

Faster and faster the Sailors rowed and faster and faster the little ship raced towards the precipitous drop. They could hear, above the constant whistling, the roar of water as it tumbled into the chasm.

'Er, people,' Knobby called from up the mast, 'I can see right down it now. It goes on forever.'

They were metres from the edge and still rowing hard. Suddenly, with a high eeking command to the rowers, Phd swung the wheel and the Lexi veered away. The Sailors rowed harder and, for a while, it seemed that they might slip sideways over the drop. Gradually the gap widened and, although their pace barely slackened, they eased away from the tempestuous boundary.

'Keep on this course,' Phd said as she handed the wheel over to the Captain. 'I have to go and help my people below. We are not safe yet.'

'But you can talk.' was all Ali could say.

'Yes, well, I will have to have a word with you about that but this is not the time.' With that she left the bridge to join her colleagues below.

Heading for Home

It was several days of hard rowing before the Lexi passed through the surrounding fog and out into more normal seas and days after that before the rowers could rest more than one at a time. The crew brought them food from the stores to keep their strength up and, exhausted as they were, they kept a steady rhythm.

Under a red sun the distant, purple coast of Uverland slipped past.

The crows resumed their lookout duties, relieving Knobby from the masthead, and the crew gathered around the galley table to discuss the situation.

'Who would believe that Sailors can talk our language?' said Digby.

'No one,' said Ali, 'that is why I didn't put it in the log.'

'So where are we now?' said Norman, stroking his wart. 'I think it is time we went home.' The others nodded in agreement.

'I have been adjusting our course to the north as much as I dare,' said the Captain, 'but I fear it is a long way.'

'At least we will have circumnavigated the globe,' said Digby, optimistically.

'If we don't starve to death first,' said Prudence, absently polishing a fork.

'We could put into Uverland for supplies,' said Digby to which a sharp intake of breath was the only response. 'Well, I am a bit curious.'

'You're on your own there,' said Norman.

'I'm game,' said Sally, but without much conviction.

'Don't you think we've had enough excitement for one year?' Norman put his arm around her.

'I suppose you're right.' She kissed him on the cheek and snuggled into his chest.

Digby frowned but he knew that the trepidation they all felt for the land of dark foreboding would prevail.

'Perhaps next trip,' said Sally brightly.

'That still leaves us with the problem of provisions,' said Prudence. 'Could we try fishing?'

'This far out, all we would do is attract the flying sharks,' said Ali, 'and I don't think we have the strength to fight off another attack.'

'Well then,' said Prudence, 'we have oil, flour and potatoes, but apart from a few carrots and scraggy cabbages there's nothing much left. We fed all the fresh vegetables to the Sailors.'

'There is a bin in the hold that is still full,' said Peter.

'Which one? said Digby.

'Bay "S" I think.'

'Sprouts,' the others muttered.

'Oh,' said Peter.

'Even the Sailors won't eat them,' said Ben.

'So potato cakes it is for the rest of the voyage,' said Prudence brightly.

They travelled on for many days. Prudence did her best with the provisions available but the diet of potato cake, potato bread, potatoes in oil, potatoes not in oil and chips with everything soon made the strict rationing become a pleasure.

At least the Sailors were at last able to jump over the side to forage for seaweed and, once their vigour returned, they rowed ever harder against the slackening current towards the north. The golden sun rose higher in the sky each day and the red one reduced its gloomy influence, eventually to be lost below the southern horizon.

However, there came a day when Prudence had to break it to the crew.

'I have good news and I have bad news,' she said over dinner of Kentucky fried potatoes. 'What do you want first?'

The response was split fifty-fifty.

'Ok . . . the bad news,' she went on. 'This is the last of the potatoes.' The crew didn't know whether cry or cheer.

'So what's the good news?' said Norman, his chin resting on his fist.

'Elbows off the table please, Norman.' Sally had gone all school matronly since she had been in charge of rationing.

Prudence went on, 'I have found a bunch of garlic.'

'Oh goody,' said Norman keeping his arms by his side. 'What're we going to put it on?'

'It's no good, we'll have to face it,' said Digby, 'it has to be the sprouts.' The depth of dismay had them all with their elbows on the table burying their faces in their hands.

Prue was first to recover. 'Perhaps with the garlic I can make them palatable.' But she didn't sound convinced.

It was agreed that an early night was in order and, despite their weakened state, they would skip breakfast, potentially being sprouts, and meet for brunch. Tummies rumbled all night long, partially from hunger and partially in fear of their next meal.

Cargo Bay "S"

It was quite early when Prudence sent Digby and Peter to fetch a sack of sprouts from cargo bay S. Sally and Norman were still in bed and Prue wondered how they found the energy to lay in so long.

'Come on Peter,' said Digby, 'let's get this over with.' He led the way down to the hold. As they removed the cover, the first sack flopped out towards them and, to their horror, the others inched forward as if to follow it. Digby thought he must still be asleep as one of his recurring nightmares unfolded before him. Attacked by rabid mutant sprouts; he backed off. Peter, his years as a pirate coming to the fore, slashed at the advancing sack with his dagger, splitting it open. Out tumbled a jumble of round creatures making a sound like waves on a beach as their shells rubbed and clattered against each other.

Peering round the edge of cargo bay "M" where they had fled, they watched as the creatures started to spread out on the floor, slowly but remorselessly heading towards them and leaving slimy trails in their wake.

'Snails,' said Digby in surprise.

'Snails?' said Peter.

'Just snails,' said Digby.

'Can you eat them?'

'I don't know, we can try . . . can't be worse than sprouts, can they? Quick gather them up before they escape.'

For a few frantic moments Digby and Peter became snail cowboys, herding the elusive critters back before corralling them in their cargo bay.

With Peter carrying the remains of the sack, loaded as much as possible with the slow-moving molluscs, they returned to the galley.

'I've got good news and bad news,' said Digby as he entered.

'Oh, give me the good news,' Prue replied with a sigh.

'We don't have any sprouts.'

Sally for a moment was filled with joy but the fleeting feeling fled quickly, "and?' she said.

'They have been eaten by these.' Digby gestured to Peter who emptied his bag onto the table.

'Oooer, Prudence jumped back in surprise.'

'Digby laughed. 'They're only snails.'

"Oh . . . well they are making slimy trails all over my nice clean table . . . get them off . . .' She grabbed a large saucepan off the stove and held it as if threatening the intruders, 'Put them in this before they escape.'

Digby and Peter scooped their charges into the iron receptacle and placed it on the stove.

Prudence slammed a lid on it quick. 'Do you expect me to cook them?' she snapped as she reached for her dishcloth. 'Look at the mess they've made.'

'We'll leave you to it, shall we?' Digby backed out the door where Peter had already fled.

Brunch was approached with considerable caution but, once they had tasted the strange dish placed before them, they had to agree that snails sauté in garlic was quite the tastiest dish they had ever had. Getting the little rascals out of their shells was a lengthy and messy business but it was so worth it.

That evening as the Sailors pulled steadily towards home, the crew sat on deck under a peaceful clear sky, for the moment at least, safe and happy. Phd joined them with a polite cough and asked if she may address them on a matter of utmost importance.

The Great Green Apes

Phd leaned against the mast and contemplated the Urlanders that sat in a semicircle around her. 'My friends,' she said, yes, we are friends, aren't we?' Heads nodded in unison. 'We have been through many adventures together but I have to confess I have committed a great indiscretion and need to ask of you a big favour.' Her voice was refined and she spoke with soft and perfect diction. 'I have revealed a secret that my people have held for generations.'

'The fact that you can speak our language,' Digby spoke gravely.

'Yes Mr Digby. I would never have spoken so if we had not been in clear and imminent danger and I fear my hormones may have had a role to play also.' She gently stroked her tummy.

'But why does it have to be a secret?' Sally asked.

'I can offer an explanation but, before I do, I must ask that you to promise not to reveal what I am about to tell you or that some of us can speak Urlandian.'

'Why don't you want to speak like us anyway?' said Ben 'instead of all that crude eeeing and hooing.'

'Our language is, in fact, much more sophisticated than yours, all be it that much of it is conducted beyond the range of your ears. It is the binary language of higher mathematics and can convey more than you can comprehend. But I have said too much. Do you agree to keep our secret if I tell you more?'

Enthralled they all murmured their assent.

'It is a long story covering many generations of your people and quite a few of my own. It goes back to a cataclysmic event in this world's past. An event which changed its nature completely. Previously, the dominant species of the planet had wasted and polluted nature so much that it was due for a shake up and, as is the way with these things, one actually happened. I will not go into details but it did threaten the existence of all. Our ancestors, yours and mine, were called "Humans" and they reacted in several ways. For us, we still think of ourselves as "Human," We re-engineered our form to cope with the changing conditions on the planet. We set a tradition of living *with* nature, not in conflict with it. Our days were spent, and still are to the most part, in peaceful contemplation of all that is beautiful and pondering the wonders of the universe. We require only vegetation to live on and offer no conflict with the eco system.

Others chose a different path. Your people, who look very similar to the ancestors, hid away in bunkers in the ground only to return to the surface when the planet stabilised again. They were aware that much of what their forefathers did all but destroyed the world, and yes, by the way, it is round. They chose to hide the technology that previously troubled the ecosystem from their children. They introduced the memory wart in an attempt to slow the headlong dash for industrial advance until your society developed the understanding to use it safely. And so we live together in peace and harmony. We have watched over you ever since. Monitoring and, on rare occasions, guiding you in your progress.

'I think that is as much as I should tell you, unless you have any specific questions.'

'Will you get into trouble for telling us this?' Sally asked.

'I do not know. This has never happened before and we have no sanctions in place for transgressors in our society.'

Captain Ali stroked his wart thoughtfully. 'Back there at the waterfall . . . you seemed to know exactly what to do. Had you done that before?'

'Not with a ship, but I once passed that way on one of our Islands.' A tear appeared in the corner of her eye and she sighed. 'On that occasion not all of us survived but we discovered the slingshot technique that I used for the Lexi.' She wiped her face with the back of her hairy hand. 'It is not a waterfall; actually it is a maelstrom, a great hole in the planet's crust. The water flows into it like going down a drain. Near the bottom it is turned to steam by the heat in the planet's core and rises up to form clouds that spread out to fall as rain to keep the sea topped up. Clever huh? . . . That is one discovery you *can* reveal in your thesis Mr Digby.'

There was a thoughtful silence for a while, broken only when Prudence asked, 'When is your baby due?'

The boys drifted away as their girlfriends gathered closer to their giant hairy friend to talk softly of matters female.

'Well, that's a turn up and no mistake,' said Norman. 'I hope no one breaks their promise. Not even in your journal, Digby.'

'Of course not,' Digby replied indignantly. 'That reminds me, I haven't written it up since that first day. Professor Ramekin will expect a report when we get back.'

'We'll do it together,' said Norman, 'starting first thing in the morning.'

No Place like Home

Morning came with a squawk, well a whole lot of them actually. The crows had seen something on the horizon. Knobby was already shinning up the mast when Norm and Dig stumbled on deck. Peter was at the wheel steering due north. Ali and Ben joined him in the wheelhouse.

'Can you see anything, Mr Mate?' Ali called out, adding an '*ahar,*' just to get back into practice.

The crows were in a flap and flapped around Knobby's head as he stood precariously on the roof of their house. 'Land Ho,' he cried excitedly. 'It's land dead ahead. Cap'n, I can see a palm tree.'

It seemed to be ages before they could see the land from the deck. Knobby came down from the crow's nest and Prudence served breakfast of snails on toast. They washed it down with tea which had to be made from scrapings from metal parts of the ship that had started to rust.

When he returned aloft it was only to report the disappointing news it was only a floating island.

'I hope it's not occupied,' 'Ali mused. I don't think I could stand another party.'

'I'll check,' said Phd. 'She cupped her hands around her mouth and, although they could hear nothing, they knew she was calling out to her people.' After listening intently for a moment she reported, 'No, no occupants,'

'Good,' said Ali, we'll put in and forage for supplies. The water situation is getting desperate.'

Phd still seemed to be listening. 'No need Captain, I have just had a message from my land-based relatives. Urland is just over the horizon. We can be there by morning.' With the happy crew gathered round she went on to say, 'This is the last time I will be able to speak to you in your language,' and, from that moment on, she never said anything more than ee or hooo. They all knew the truth about the Great Green Apes now but never spoke of it again.

And so it was. They had arrived a week's travel along the coast from where they started and, once they purchased supplies with the last of their college fund and sent an internet eagle message to their parents, it was a pleasant cruise home. Captain Ali and Knobby dropped the adventurers off in the harbour and immediately set off for the nearest floating island for a change of Sailors so that Phd could have her baby in peace. Peter decided not to go back to the law and became a permanent member of the Lexi's crew. Sally went home to plan a wedding to the secret delight of Norm. Ben wrote the definitive gourmet cheese cookbook and was accepted back into the proud Kipling family.

Prudence perfected her recipe for Garlic Snails and named it after the hold where they were discovered. It became a firm favourite in her parents' restaurant appearing on the menu as "S-Cargo."

Digby filled his exercise book with their discoveries and adventures He thought of calling it

"Around the World in Eighty Days" but had the niggling impression it had been done before so settled on **"Norm and Dig's Epic Adventure"**

About the creators of Norm and Dig's.

Story:

John Goodwin: Born, London, in 1947. Married, Jean in 1969. Two sons; one granddaughter.

John took a break from writing crime thrillers to write an exciting adventure story for younger reader. However it was not untill he found a great illustrator that he felt able to publish it.

It is now supported by a collection of his short stories as an E Book also for younger readers.

His first novel 'The Last Olympiad' was long listed in the *2008 Opening Pages competition*; now published by Anixe publishing Ltd, as was his second, "Slow Hand."

Other writing credits: international poetry competition runners up prize, various articles, poems and short stories, published in Cyprus. He also wrote a monthly column for Property World until the magazine failed in 2009.

Future projects: Publication of his back catalogue of short stories, for adults this time, in an anthology called "Take a Look in my Shorts." Then more crime fiction.

Illustrator:

Adrian Waygood: Born, Swansea, in 1946. Married to Anita.

Retired electrical engineer, naval officer, and educator. Author of two engineering textbooks, *'An Introduction to Electrical Science'* and *'Electrical Technology for Technicians'*, published by Routledge.

Amateur illustrator: mainly technical, together with theatrical posters and programmes, until approached by John to create cartoon characters to illustrate his children's book.

Future projects include a new engineering textbook, *'Symmetrical Components –Simply Explained!'*

Lightning Source UK Ltd.
Milton Keynes UK
UKHW021317101118
332114UK00005B/21/P